Do You Take This Man?

by

Jacquie May Miller

This is a work of fiction. Names, characters, places, and incidents are either the product of the author's imagination or are used fictitiously, and any resemblance to actual persons living or dead, business establishments, events, or locales is entirely coincidental.

Do You Take This Man?

COPYRIGHT © 2023 by Jacquie May Miller

Cover Art by *The Wild Rose Press, Inc.*

The Wild Rose Press, Inc.
PO Box 708
Adams Basin, NY 14410-0708
Visit us at www.thewildrosepress.com

Publishing History
First Edition, 2023
Trade Paperback ISBN 978-1-5092-5069-1
Digital ISBN 978-1-5092-5070-7

Published in the United States of America

Dedication

To my sister and best friend, Sue. Thank you for always being there for me. You are the one person who will recognize the heart of our dad in the character of Jack Madison. Love you.

Chapter One

I do

Try as he might, Jack could not keep his gaze fixed on Mary's emerald-green eyes—not that he didn't love those eyes with all his being—they'd been the first of her many features to capture his heart. But today the view a little farther south demanded his attention as Mary's lacey bra peeked over the stretched white fabric of her dress—pushing her ample bosom starkly into Jack's field of vision. Despite the distraction, he heard the captain's voice, jerked his head upward and answered the question he'd been itching to answer:

"I do!"

Jack's voice was strong and steady as he pledged his commitment, but what he really wanted to shout at the top of his lungs was, "You're God damn right, I do!" He kept his words to the script out of respect for his new bride, but in his heart, he knew, Mary would love him no matter what he said. How had he gotten so lucky?

The warm tropical breeze played with the thinning patch of gray hairs scattered across Jack's head as he watched that same breeze blow the skirt of Mary's white silk dress straight up to her neck in Marilyn Monroe fashion—revealing her red lace panties. Getting married on the bow of a cruise ship had its shortcomings, but one look at the reflection of the warm Mexican sun on the ocean waves told him this had been the right choice. Who was he kidding? He wasn't looking at the waves; he was looking at those red panties even as he helped her push the flowing skirt back down to her knees. The small group of spectators let out a gasp, then a giggle. Mary didn't even blush—Jack had learned she was not ashamed of her body even though her thighs looked more like peach colored crepe paper than the firm stalks of her youth. Jack loved every inch of her—the bottle-red curls, the creases surrounding her green Irish eyes, and especially the soft curves of her mature hourglass figure. He couldn't get enough of her and in a few minutes, she would be his wife.

"Do you, Mary Bradley, take this man, Jack Madison, to be your husband, in sickness and in health, forsaking all others as long as you both shall live?"

Mary winked at the man who was about to become her husband. "You bet your sweet ass I do!"

The captain laughed along with the rest of the family. "Jack, I think this woman is ready for the honeymoon. Slip on that ring and kiss your bride."

Jack put his hands on Mary's rosy cheeks and kissed her as if no one was watching—then he put the ring on her finger. The captain hadn't specified the order of things and if Jack had waited another moment to kiss his bride, his heart would have burst. Taking her newly adorned hand, he turned to the few guests, raised their clasped hands in victory, and started walking toward his family.

"Not so fast, buddy." Mary's first words as Mrs. Madison were a bit harsh. "Give me that hand so I can put a ring on it. I don't want there to be any question that you're taken." He offered his left hand to accept the object that would mark him as forbidden fruit.

"Don't you trust me, dear?" He tried to sound indignant but, truthfully, he was happy to be "taken" by his sweet Mary.

"I do. Especially now that you're marked with that gold band." She threw her head back, laughing as he repeated the victory fist pump with their intertwined fingers.

Jack couldn't imagine a better day. He and Mary were poised to walk down the aisle, but there wasn't an aisle—just ten folding chairs holding their closest family members.

The oldest guest, Jack's Aunt Dorothy, or Dot as she preferred to be called, lifted her eighty-five-year-old butt off the hard, white lattice chair and shouted, "To the bar!" That's where the reception, if you could call it that, would set the tone for the marriage of Jack and Mary Madison.

Mary's son, Sam, handed her the bouquet of red roses she'd set aside as she spoke her vows. Sam was like a son to Jack, not only because he was Mary's son, but because he was actually his son-in-law. If Sam and Jamie hadn't pushed him to call Mary two years ago, he might still be a bitter, grieving widower. That call saved his life and now here he was experiencing life as he had never known it. Before Mary, life was a chore—after Mary, well, after Mary life blossomed like the roses in her bouquet, each petal adding a new layer of happiness he hadn't thought possible.

Sam hugged his mom, holding her tightly as he whispered, "Love you, Mom." Then he reached for Jack, hugging him with the same intensity. "Congratulations, you two! Jack, you better treat my mom right." Although the words could have been generic, Jack knew the deep scar that marked both Sam and Mary.

"You know I will, Sam." Yes, he would treat them both right, not like that bastard, Vernon Bradley. Thank God Mary had finally left that asshole. "Aren't you ever going to call me Dad?"

"The last guy I called Dad left a bad taste in my mouth. You know I think of you like a father, but I'll have to come up with a different name for you."

"Fair enough." Jack then turned to his youngest daughter, Jamie. "You got yourself a good man, sweetie."

"Just like my dad!" Jamie smiled as she adjusted eighteen-month-old Dorothy Rose on her hip. Rosie, as they all called her, reached for her grandpa as Jamie used her other arm to wrap him in a hug. Mary leaned in, lifting Rose to her chest.

"Thank you, sweetie, and thanks for giving us this beautiful granddaughter. I'm going to be here to watch this one grow up." Jack still had a hard time forgiving himself for missing the childhood of Jamie's older son, Justin. He was lucky his daughter and grandson had given him a second chance.

Everything felt like a new beginning after his first wife, Nancy, died two years ago. Nancy had pushed everyone out of their lives who didn't follow her rules and Jamie had been a casualty of her unyielding moral code. Jack didn't agree with Nancy but had been manipulated into going along with the twenty-five-year estrangement from their youngest daughter. The sadness he felt when Nancy died was real—he had loved that difficult woman—even feeling compassion for her as she played the "poor me" card over and over again. He was surprised how bright his world became once Nancy was gone—the dark cloud of anxiety and guilt finally lifted. Jamie's forgiveness parted the clouds, but his introduction to Sam's mom, Mary, removed the clouds altogether, blinding him with brilliant sunshine. That was how love was supposed to feel. He knew that now.

Jack turned his eyes from his bride to the line of relatives descending upon them with the promise of more hugs and good wishes. Thank God the family was small, or they'd be standing there all day. He was ready for champagne, but not before his final hug for his oldest daughter. No one knew better than Sarah what he had endured with his late wife, Nancy. As their first child, Sarah had been present for all but six months of their marriage—indeed the reason for their hasty wedding—and had lived nearby even after leaving home. What would he have done without her? She leaned toward his good ear.

"I'm so happy for you, Dad. The change in you these past two years just blows my mind." Jack held her hand as she spoke. "You used to be so quiet around Mom, but now—now you can't stop chattering. It's great to see you so happy." Sarah turned her gaze to the woman responsible for the transformation. "Thanks, Mary."

"You don't need to thank me. Bringing him back to life was my pleasure." She touched Jack's cheek, guiding his mouth to her ruby red lips. Her eyes, like green emeralds, locked onto his as she spoke. "I wasn't exactly the life of the party when we met, either."

"We bring out the best in each other," Jack said as he remembered how quiet they had both been on their first date. Jack was used to Nancy's wrath whenever he made a remark that didn't coincide with her agenda.

Luckily, she only beat him verbally. Mary kept quiet to avoid physical harm—a dissenting opinion in her household usually led to a slap at best and often a fist if she got too lippy. When Jack and Mary got together they cautiously tested the waters with an opinion here and a smart remark there and found their words were not only accepted, but truly appreciated.

"I knew you had it in you, Dad. When Mom's back was turned, I got a glimpse of your wicked sense of humor. Now you can say whatever the hell you want, and it seems you're doing just that," Sarah said.

Sarah's husband, David, had been standing quietly by her side. Now he spoke. "I married into a family with no filters." He rolled his eyes. "I take that back. The filters were on high when Nancy was alive, but now you've all come out of your shells. Don't get me wrong—I like it. I'm just trying to adjust."

"Oh, David, you're just as wild as the rest of us in your own quiet way." Sarah smiled, then shot him a wink. The color rising in her face led Jack to believe David's wild side was saved mostly for her. She took a deep breath, fanned her face, and regained her composure. "So, let's get down to the lounge. They've got an area set up for us for your reception."

"I'm ready. Let's go, sweetie." Jack took Mary's hand and pressed it to his lips.

Mary looked at the one guest still seated, her son, Robert. "You go ahead, dear. I'll be there in a few minutes."

Jack followed her eyes to the man sitting quietly in the last chair. Robert was not like his brother, Sam. While Sam had rejected his father completely, Robert still kept Vern Bradley in his family circle often defending him over his mother. He was a hard one to warm up to, but Jack understood the dynamics of the abused and hoped Robert would see the light one of these days.

"Don't let him bring you down. This is our day," Jack said.

"I know, but I want him to feel included. Even if he insists on continuing his relationship with Vern, I want him to know I'm still there for him. Forgiveness is a good thing. I've forgiven Vern—I have to if I want to be free of him."

"You're a better person than I am, Mary Madison." He kissed her forehead. "Ah, I like the way that sounds."

"I'm not such a good person. I've forgiven the man—if it weren't for him, I wouldn't have my sons. But I'm not sure I can forgive myself for letting him hurt those boys." Her smile was long gone at this point. "Vern convinced me they needed discipline and back then people spanked their children. I just didn't know it was that bad. The boys never told me how much pain they were in. I thought he saved all the big hits for me."

"And I'm sure you thought you deserved it, but you know better now. You deserve the best—me!" Jack wrapped his arms around his wife, holding her tight enough to squeeze the guilt out of her. She didn't need to visit that arena of self-doubt and blame again. "I'm not sure I can truly forgive Nancy for how she treated me and my girls and I'm damn sure I'll never forgive your ex-husband for the abuse he inflicted on you and your boys."

"Speaking of my boys, let me go talk to Robert. I'll be down in a minute."

"Okay. Don't be too long." Jack headed for the

7

staircase as Mary made her way to her firstborn son. Jack stood in the shadows as he watched Mary comfort her son, her arm around his shoulder as he bowed his head. Was he angry or sad? So hard to tell—and if Jack was honest with himself, he wasn't comfortable leaving Mary alone with the man. She was blinded by her motherly instincts, but Jack saw a different side of Robert. He was a bit too quiet for this family, so he was either severely depressed from his years of abuse or severely disturbed. Either way, he made Jack nervous— he would stay nearby for now. As he watched them stand up, he headed down the staircase hoping she wouldn't catch him eavesdropping.

****

Jack ran through the door of the lounge and planted himself in front of his grandson, Justin, and his fiancée Annie. Jack could barely catch his next breath, but he stood as still as possible, trying not to let his heaving chest give him away.

"Hey, you two, if Mary asks, we've been talking for a while, okay?"

"Sure, Grandpa. What's going on?" Justin handed Jack his glass of champagne to make it look like he'd been there long enough to start partying.

"Oh, I was just spying on my new bride." He unbuttoned his tuxedo jacket and bent over taking in a deep breath. "Whoa, I ran down the stairs as soon as I saw her and Robert walking toward the stairway. I'm not sure I have the wind for this at sixty-nine."

Annie laughed. "You better get in shape, Grandpa Jack. Mary's only sixty-five and she looks like a ball of fire."

"Oh, don't I know it. I have plenty of wind for my

Mary. Running—not so much."

Jack took a big swig of champagne as he watched Mary enter the room with Robert. They were smiling even if a bit somber. Why that man was so sullen and unpleasant was beyond Jack. His brother had endured the same upbringing and he was hopeful and optimistic— hard to believe they were raised in the same home. But if anyone could soften his heart, Mary would be the one.

"Hey, old man." Mary patted Jack's backside as she walked into the conversational circle. "Did you miss me?"

"Of course. I've been waiting patiently for you, dear." He wrapped his arm around her waist. "C'mon, Robert, come join us."

Robert gave Jack a half smile. Even after two years of Jack's presence in his mother's life, Robert still hadn't warmed up to the idea of someone replacing his father. "Thanks, but I think I'll go get myself a drink." He nodded and walked away.

"What did he have to say to you?" Jack asked.

"Oh, nothing much. We can talk about it later. Now, I want to have a glass of champagne and cut that beautiful cake."

Justin spoke up—he had the loudest, deepest voice so everyone jumped when he raised his voice. "Hey, everybody, it's time for cake. And there's plenty more champagne. Nobody has to drive home, so let's party!"

The group was small, but energetic, clapping and "woohooing" over to the corner where the small, but elegant white cake sat in a bed of rose petals. The obligatory plastic couple adorned the top, but these figures were more "mature" with hands in the air that appeared to be throwing rose petals off the top of the

9

cake. Rich red icing formed roses and stray petals that cascaded from the plastic hands down the imaginary trail to the base of the cake—the delicate frosting blending with the live flowers.

"I'm not sure I want to cut this. Did anyone get a picture?"

Sam piped up. "We all did, Mom, and we're all waiting for you two to make the first cut so we can take more. Don't worry, you'll have a Facebook page full of pictures in a couple of days."

Mary held the knife, Jack covering her hand with his, but before they made the cut, a voice from the past froze their hand and silenced the joyful noise around them.

"What the hell do you think you're doing, Mary Bradley? You can't marry that son of a bitch. You're still married to me!" Vern was moving closer, his six-foot-two frame closing the space between them far too quickly.

"What do you mean? We've been divorced for almost two years."

"Not in the eyes of the church, we're not. Catholics can't get divorced. Don't you remember your religious upbringing? You made me convert to your damn religion and now I'm cashing in on the Pope's words." Vern took another step toward the newlyweds.

"Hold it right there, Vern. I've got a big ass knife in my hand, so don't come any closer or I'll use it, I swear." She pulled the knife free from Jack's hand and raised it high. "You never gave a damn about the church when we were married. You don't get to find religion when it's convenient."

"I got a piece of paper that says you're going to be

excommunicated if you leave me."

"I don't give two shits about the church anymore. They never gave me any help when you were using me for your personal punching bag. They can't kick me out—I quit!"

"You're surely going to hell, Mary." He moved closer, obviously not afraid of the knife that was now within striking distance of his oversized beer gut.

"I lived in Hell for over forty years. The church might not agree, but the State says I'm rid of you, so get the hell out of here." She lowered her hand.

"You'll never be rid of me." Vern's voice softened as he knelt down. Mary noticed he'd worn his best white shirt and the cheesy stars and stripes tie she'd threatened to throw out numerous times. As he took his hand and slicked back his mop of unruly dyed black hair, his voice cracked. "I love you, Mary. I can't live without you."

"Oh, spare me. You should have thought of that before you beat the love out of me."

"I didn't mean to hurt you, Mary. You just made me so mad. I couldn't help it."

"What made you the maddest, Vern? Dinner being five minutes late, or my inability to stop the boys from crying? Or maybe it made you mad when I didn't have time to put on makeup before you got home. But you got even madder when I wore too much makeup. So, what the fuck was it, Vern?" She dropped the knife and walked over to him—on his knees he was about her height. "I'm pretty tempted to stick my pointy red shoe in your groin, but maybe I'll settle for this." She wanted to return the abuse he'd dished out over the years, but as she lifted her hand to deliver a slap, she stopped. She wouldn't stoop to his level.

"Don't even think about it, bitch!" Vern grabbed her wrist—she winced with the pain of his tight hold. He stood to his full height, towering over his former wife, his grip sure to leave a bruise. It wouldn't be the first time he'd left his mark on her.

"Let her go." Jack bellowed as he reached for Mary's hand prompting Vern to drop it like it was a hot potato.

"I was just trying to stop her from doing something she'd be sorry for. I don't want to hurt her. You're the one who needs to go."

"Is that a threat?" Jack knew he was asking for trouble, but out of the corner of his eye he saw Justin and Sam ready to back him up.

"No, it's a promise." Vern stepped closer and looked down at Jack's wiry five-foot-nine frame. "Stay away from my wife or you'll be sorry."

Jack stood as tall as he could and only came up to Vern's nose. He looked up. "She's my wife now, asshole. You better keep your distance if you know what's good for you."

"And what if I don't know what's good for me?" Vern set his big, calloused hand on Jack's head, reminding him he was no match for Mary's bigger, stronger ex-husband. As Sam and Justin moved toward him, Vern pulled his hand away.

"That's enough, Vern. Get over it. I'm not coming back, so get the hell out of here." Mary grabbed Jack's hand and pulled him back toward the cake. Vern didn't move. "I said, get out—now!" He moved toward her again and she picked up the knife. "Don't even think about hitting me again. Or maybe I should let you. I've got witnesses this time."

"Okay, okay, I'm leaving, but this isn't over." Vern turned to leave, then looked over his shoulder, his eyes locking onto hers. "You better watch your back, bitch."

Jack jerked forward, but Mary held him back. "You don't talk about my wife that way. If you come near her, you better sleep with one eye open, buddy, because I swear, I'll kill you if you touch her again."

Chapter Two

The Life of the Party

"Sorry, Mom. I should have stepped up and confronted Dad," Sam said. "I think we were all in shock, but I'm glad to see you're not taking any shit from him. Are you okay?"

"I'm just fine. I'm not going to let him ruin this day. Come on, everyone, let's have some cake." She took the knife and she and Jack cut the first piece. "So, take a picture already." Jack and Mary pulled the red and white slice of cake apart and fed each other the first bite. Everyone took a picture.

Sam was right, the family was in shock. But Mary snapped them out of their stupor passing out cake and champagne. Even as she kept her brave face, she wondered why Vern had suddenly decided to fight her new marriage. He'd been quiet for over a year—a sign, she thought, he had accepted his fate. Something wasn't adding up. For some reason, she wasn't afraid of the man—she'd enjoyed flashing the knife at the old goat, but there was no danger there. Forty plus years of living with Vern Bradley had honed her radar and this was not a credible threat—this was a show of some kind. What the hell was he up to?

"Come on, everybody. Snap out of it. Time for some dancing. Who's going to choose our first song? The

Karaoke machine is waiting."

"I got this, Mom." Sam gave Jamie a kiss and took the stage. "This is a song about loving someone long after our youth is gone." As he started to sing *Thinking Out Loud*, Mary felt the words were perfect for her and Jack, and as the song said, she couldn't wait to kiss Jack *under the light of a thousand stars*. From the tone in her son's voice, it was clear Sam felt the same love—the kind of love that transcends age—for his wife. Mary had no doubt Sam and Jamie would be one of the lucky couples, loving through the loss of hair, eyesight, hearing, and the addition of wrinkles, pounds, and aching joints. Love was not just for the young and as she and Jack danced to the lyrics flowing so beautifully from Sam's throat, she felt the love in Jack's touch. As his hand caressed the small of her back, her spine tingled in anticipation of their wedding night—not that she hadn't been in his bed before. But tonight was different and while sixty-five years was a long time to wait for love, it had been worth the wait. As the song ended, Mary kissed her man as she held his face in her aging hands. Jack returned the kiss pulling those lovely old hands from his wrinkled cheeks. Mary would have liked to linger there awhile, but Jack gave her his signature wink, kissed her palms, and left her on the dance floor as he joined Sam at the Karaoke machine. Once on the stage, she saw him whisper in Sam's ear and within moments, the intro to the next song brought sighs of recognition.

"C'mon David, Justin. You, too, Robert. This is a song for our women," Jack shouted before the first line. Justin and David took the bait and joined Jack and Sam. Then Jack began. "I've got sunshine…" He finished the line then handed the microphone to David who crooned the next line of the classic song, "My Girl". From there, Sam and Justin joined in.

The guys made a good effort to look like the Temptations, moving from side to side, twirling their arms and kicking their legs like chorus girls. Robert stood aside choosing not to join them but cracked the smallest of smiles as the boys performed for their girls.

"I love this song. Come on, Robert, come dance with your mom." Mary moved toward her eldest son, twirling until she was face to face with his stony countenance, the involuntary curve of his lips fading. "Put down your drink and snap out of your funk, Bobby. I want to see a smile on your face, God damn it." She grabbed his hand and pulled him onto the dance floor.

He smiled per his mother's instructions and then laughed as he grabbed her around the waist and spun her around the floor. Mary was ecstatic—her husband was singing to her, and her first-born son was finally joining the party. Maybe there was hope for Robert after all. She had to believe that—she couldn't bear to think he was becoming a clone of his father. It was fine that he looked like his dad, the thick dark hair and dark lashes reminded her of Vern in his younger days—the Vern she once found so attractive. No, she didn't mind that Robert looked like Vern, but it seemed her son was starting to act like the old bastard; she would never let that happen. She owed Robert her life and now it was her turn to save him.

It was just a dance, but she saw a change in her son as he guided her across the room. He was a wonderful dancer and for the first time in two years, his perpetually furrowed brow relaxed. Mary's flowing white skirt floated through the air as Robert lifted her hand allowing her to twirl her geriatric body under the arch of their grip. As he brought her back toward him, she noticed how handsome he looked in his charcoal gray suit, the blue and gray checked tie bringing out the blue in his eyes— and he was smiling. She hoped someone was taking a picture of this.

As the song ended, they turned and applauded the boys on their fine performance. Mary was beaming, not only because of the guys on stage, but because of Robert's obvious joy. "Thank you, Robert. I needed to see your smile again." She kept her right hand in his, using the left to reach up and brush a lock of dark hair from his forehead. "I remember teaching you to dance when you were twelve years old. Now, look at you. You're a regular Fred Astaire."

"Aw, Mom." His smile was starting to fade, as he took a deep breath. "I guess I still like to dance. It's everything else that's all fucked up."

"Everything will be fine, honey. I know this has been hard for you, but don't you want your old mom to be happy?"

"Not with Jack. He's just using you. Can't you see that?" His eyes narrowed as his frown returned. "You're taking Dad's money and giving it to that old fart."

"It's not like that. Your dad owes me something for raising his kids, cooking his meals, and all the other obligations of being his wife. He wouldn't let me work you know."

"That's not what he says."

"Well, it's the truth. And Jack doesn't care about my money. He has a good retirement. He's not rich, but we do just fine." Mary dropped her son's hand. "But I don't want to have this conversation now. Let's go get some food."

It was almost 7:00 p.m. Sam and Jamie had arranged a personal buffet for the wedding party and after all the excitement—not to mention the dancing—Mary had worked up an appetite. The aroma of prime rib, roasted potatoes, tropical fruits, and various side dishes swirled into one heavenly scent that made her stomach beg to be filled. She put her arm around Robert, hoping to pull him back into that happy place they enjoyed only a few minutes ago. It was too late.

"I'm not that hungry. You go ahead." He turned away and headed to the other side of the lounge where other passengers had gathered. What was he doing? He walked to the bar and sat next to an attractive woman who appeared to be in her late thirties. Did he know her? He was either coming on strong to a strange woman or they were already well acquainted. Mary guessed the latter. If he had a girlfriend, why hadn't he brought her to the wedding? Maybe it was time for her to let go and let Robert be Robert. Where was the boy she raised, the boy who clung to his mother and protected her? At times, it seemed like he had raised her as they traveled through the dark years of abuse. As she withdrew and lost her sense of self, Robert became stronger and more responsible, often shielding her from her husband's powerful fist.

Now the tables had turned as she took back her life and emerged from the dark cocoon that had held her hostage for too many years. Although Robert should have been happy to see her escape, he didn't seem to be ready for the strong, kick-ass butterfly that was busting out of that cocoon. He had never seen that side of his mom and if Mary were to guess, she would have said he wasn't ready to give up his role as protector. Maybe he was just a little bit controlling himself—a gene he likely inherited from Vern.

As her mind followed the trail back to her early years with Vern and Robert, she found herself standing alone in the middle of the dance floor paralyzed. She couldn't let go of Robert even as she felt a deep sense of loss. Soon he'd be out of her life completely if he continued on his current path.

Jack snapped her out of her catatonic state. "Hey, sweetie, let's go eat. You're gonna need your strength if you want to keep up with me tonight."

"I've got as much stamina as you, dear, but a few oysters might not be a bad idea." She smiled at her new husband, the joy bubbling up within her once again. All the problems with Robert would have to be relegated to the back burner for the rest of the night, and frankly, the rest of this cruise. As Jack took her hand and led her to the buffet, she glanced over her shoulder hoping to connect with Robert one last time, but he wasn't there. The woman, still sitting at the bar, turned her head quickly before Mary's eyes caught hers. There was something familiar about her.

"Mary, I know you love your son, but you have to let him go for now. I'm sure he'll come around in time." As she turned away from the mystery woman and back toward Jack, he kissed her forehead.

"You're probably right. I don't understand why he has such a problem with you, but then I don't know how anyone could feel anything but love for you."

Jack dropped her hand and wrapped his arms around her. "I love you, Mary. Why you married me I'll never know."

"I married you because you're the kindest man I've ever known. I love you, Jack Madison." She pulled his face toward hers and planted a soft, sensuous kiss on his waiting lips. "You taste wonderful, dear, but I think I'm going to pass out if I don't get some food." Her stomach growled as they strolled to the buffet.

They filled their plates with the exquisite mix of hearty prime rib, garlic mashed potatoes, and delectable sides, including the aphrodisiac infused oysters. Sitting with their family, laughter and joy flowing as easily as the champagne, Mary did her best to focus on all the good people in her life. She stood, raising her glass, and let her words show her love.

"This day has been a bit of a wild ride, but I'm so happy to be part of this family. Thank you, Sam and Jamie, for introducing me to the man I've been waiting for all my life. And thanks for arranging this cruise and this beautiful reception for all of us. This is truly the best day of my life."

Jack stood up and tapped his glass against hers. "And the best day of *my* life." He kissed his bride, and everyone raised their glasses in agreement. "Now, let's eat some of those oysters." He winked and patted Mary's pleasingly round backside.

****

Jack hadn't been so brave with his late wife, Nancy. If he had patted her ass in public—a gesture Jack intended as an act of love—she would have slapped his hand and increased the space between them. He knew this for a fact as he had tried it, but only once. The silent treatment had followed—at least until she got him alone—then she cut him to shreds with her sharp tongue.

But Nancy was gone, and he'd been fortunate to find

a woman who was everything Nancy was not—his beautiful, sweet Mary. Yes, her tongue was a little loose and she wasn't sweet in the conventional sense, but she was kind and loving and if she said "shit" or "God damn it" now and then it didn't detract one bit from her sweet nature.

With Mary in his life, he felt like the luckiest man alive. He enjoyed the feast, making sure he consumed just the right number of oysters and when the plates were empty and the joy of the family had been infused in his heart, he made his break. He whispered to Mary "I'll be right back, sweetie. I still have one habit I can't seem to break—I need my after-dinner cigar. I won't be too long."

"If you must." She gave him a little frown, but she couldn't hold the downward turn of her lips and it turned into a smile. "I didn't sign up to change you. I just hope you don't kill yourself with those things." She kissed him and off he went. He looked back at his one true love, then walked up the stairs to the scene of the wedding ceremony. The chairs had been folded and set aside, so the aisle they'd walked down only a few hours ago no longer existed. He strode toward the railing.

Jack looked out into the darkness and the sky seemed to sparkle with the light of a thousand stars. He lit his fine cigar, inhaling the aroma he found invigorating—apparently, he was the only one. All his life he'd been relegated to remote outside locations to enjoy his long-held habit. He actually didn't mind—he enjoyed the solitude and the chance to reflect on the fateful twists and turns that brought him to this life-affirming day. He was so deeply in love with Mary his head was spinning.

Of course, he had known love before, but it was a different kind of love—love and gratitude for his family. His daughter, Sarah and her husband, David, had been there for him when Nancy died, but more than that, they had been there for him while she was alive—a much harder road than the one to the funeral home. When Sarah came into the world, Jack finally understood what love was all about. He had no idea a child could steal his heart and show him that unconditional love was possible. His beautiful hazel eyed Sarah looked exactly like Nancy, but her kind heart was nothing like her mother's.

And, then there was Jamie. He couldn't believe he'd missed more than half of her life and the entire childhood of his grandson, Justin. Nancy had done a good job of convincing Jack that Jamie wanted to break ties when she left for college with Justin barely the size of a pea in her womb. At the same time, Nancy had devised a plan that led Jamie to believe her father no longer wanted contact with her. Nancy was a master puppeteer, pulling the strings to guide the puppets to her chosen destination. Jack and Jamie didn't even know they were being played—they just followed the clues and assumed the other was severing ties. Even though twenty-five years passed without contact, he never stopped loving his baby girl—the girl with the brown eyes and chestnut brown hair that matched his—before it started falling out. It had only been two years since they re-connected, two years that changed everything. If Jamie hadn't come home, he would never have known his grandson, Justin—a boy, now a man of twenty-six, who not only looked like Jack, but shared his quirky sense of humor. And, of course, if Jamie had not fallen in love with Sam, Jack would never have met Sam's mom. That would have been a tragedy.

He sighed and took a puff of his cigar, the aroma mingling with the salty sea air. Mary might not have appreciated the mix, but to Jack it was intoxicating. Life was good—no, life was great! Smiling as he faced the open sea, he realized he hadn't been this happy in years.

The ship was sailing toward Puerto Vallarta at a good clip and the breeze was blowing what was left of Jack's hair sideways. The dull roar of the massive boat traveling through the sea was powerful, yet peaceful— he felt relaxed now that the night's earlier clash with Vern was behind him.

"Bet you thought you were rid of me," Vern said. Jack hadn't heard him walk up behind him, but at the sound of his voice he turned with a start. "You're pretty jumpy. Do I make you nervous, Jack?"

"You just surprised me. You don't make me nervous, just God damn mad." Jack was, indeed, nervous, but didn't plan on giving Vern the satisfaction of knowing the effect he had on him. With his back to the railing, Jack's palms began to sweat with anticipation—he needed to put some distance between himself and the ocean below. "I'd love to talk, but I gotta get back to my family."

"Not so fast." Vern stretched his arm out, grabbed Jack's throat, and pushed him against the rail. "I'm sick and tired of you and my pathetic excuse for a wife bleeding me dry."

"She's not your wife anymore." Jack's voice was a whisper as he struggled to talk with the heavy hand on his throat. Straining to breathe, anger rose within him, and he shoved his knee firmly into Vern's groin causing him to loosen his grip and drop his hands to his crotch.

"You son of a bitch." Vern moaned. Jack moved

from the rail leaving Vern's back to the open sea. Before Jack could get away Vern's hand rose from his genitals and his fist found Jack's face sending Jack flying. If he'd have had any sense he would have run, but with adrenaline flowing he went back for more.

Clearly, he couldn't get a punch off—Vern's long arms would stop him before he reached his target. So Jack lowered his head and charged Vern. If he was lucky, the bastard would get his due and would fall overboard— problem solved. A guttural sound rose from Jack's throat as he rushed toward Vern and as his head made contact with the big, soft belly he watched his opponent fall backward.

What had he done? He would never know because as Vern fell back, something caught Jack's foot and he fell face down on the hard deck unconscious.

****

"Jack!" Mary fell to her knees and touched his face. He stirred—he was alive. He rolled over to reveal a swollen eye and large bruise forming on his forehead. "What the hell happened? Are you all right?" She cupped his head in her hands and kissed his bloody face.

"Vern," Jack whispered and closed his eyes again.

She watched his face grow pale as she felt his slowing pulse. Was he going to die on her on the day they were just starting their lives together? She didn't want to leave his side, yet she needed help. "Help us. Somebody, please help!" Mary screamed.

Robert was the first to come to her aid. "Mom, what happened?"

"Go get Sam and help me get Jack to the ship's doctor."

Robert kneeled next to Mary. "Oh, Mom, he's okay.

It's just a couple of bruises. What happened to him anyway? Did he trip over his own feet?"

"Your father beat the crap out of him. Now get your brother and let's get him to the doctor. What happened to your compassion, Robert? Who *are* you?" Mary leaned down to cradle Jack's battered head. "Go! Hurry!"

Robert sauntered toward the stairs, but that was as far as he had to go. Sam had obviously heard his mother's scream. The whole family, in fact, was at the top of the stairs.

Jamie and Sarah ran to their father. Mary felt the color drain from her face and looking at Jack's girls she saw she was not alone.

"Am I dying? From the expressions on your faces, if I didn't know better, I'd say you girls were looking into my casket." With Mary's help, he lifted his head and leaned on his elbows to sit up. "I'm fine, girls." His eyes rolled as he swayed. "Well, maybe not fine. I do have a pretty nasty headache."

"Let's get you patched up, dear. Then, I'm going to find Vern and get this settled once and for all."

"No, Mary, please don't." Jack's voice was getting stronger as he protested her plan.

"Why not?" Her tone was more strident with each word. "He wouldn't dare hurt me with all these witnesses. It's time he got a dose of his own medicine."

Looking into Jack's glassy eyes, Mary thought about the man who had likely done the damage to her new husband. She'd given over forty years to Vern Bradley and now that she was finally moving on, he continued to stir up trouble. Would she ever be free of his shit? From the day she met that charismatic young man forty-seven years ago to the day she left him two years ago, life had been a series of assaults on both her body and her self-esteem. And now he was delivering his blows to Jack.

She thought back to the day she met Vern at a high school dance. He was the answer to her prayers—or so she thought at the tender age of eighteen. Mary had no idea then that the reason he arrived at this private Catholic school had nothing to do with his religious beliefs and everything to do with the fact that he'd been kicked out of public school for fighting and bullying. All she knew on that fateful night was that he had a gorgeous head of thick, dark hair and the bluest eyes she'd ever seen—and he wanted her.

In her quest to escape from her strict Catholic home, she jumped from the proverbial frying pan into the fire. While she willingly and happily gave herself to the handsome, young Vern Bradley, he did nothing but take. He took everything Mary had to offer—and more. Her virginity topped the list and with the ensuing pregnancy, he took her freedom.

For a good Catholic girl, there was only one option. She married Vern Bradley for better or for worse, until "death do us part." Death—that was the only way out of a Catholic marriage. She was in this for life and as much as she thought she loved Vern, she was beginning to wonder if her prayers had actually been answered. She'd been saved from the nunnery, but at what cost?

Yes, her life wasn't exactly as she had planned, but she had Robert. Even as she cursed the circumstances of his birth, she couldn't get enough of him and often clung to her beautiful baby boy, inhaling the sweet scent of baby powder and aromatic baby burps. Had she smothered the poor boy? Had he sensed her anxiety? Sometimes she held him so tight he let out a whimper and now, forty-six years later, he let out a roar.

Chapter Three

Robert's Obsession

"Where the hell is my dad?" Robert's words filled the air with their deep, resonant tone—a roar his family had seen all too often when he was angered. "You say my dad hit you. What did you do to him?"

Robert knew exactly what had happened. He'd seen the whole thing, but he wasn't ready to divulge the truth. It turned out exactly as he'd hoped, but if anyone knew he was watching in the wings it might cast suspicion on him. No, he'd wait. He'd keep his mouth shut—unless they needed a witness to Jack's assault on Vern. It wasn't likely that he'd have to come forward, after all, it was pretty cut and dried. Jack and Vern had a fight on the deck and now Vern was gone, game over.

Jack shook his head, then moaned as he brought both hands to his forehead and winced.

"Stop stalling. What happened?" Moving closer, his gaze piercing Jack's glassy, concussed eyes, Robert hovered over his prey.

Mary rose to break the eye contact and grabbed her son's arm. "Don't be so damn dramatic. What makes you think Jack did anything to your father? You know your dad well enough to know he probably punched Jack and got the hell out of here."

"Maybe Jack knows where he went." Robert's tone

was accusing. "You were the last to see him, Jack. Where do you think he is?"

"I-I-I don't know. I don't remember," Jack said in a quivering voice, barely audible even to those closest to him.

"Bullshit. Don't play dumb with me. You couldn't have lost your memory with one punch," Robert said, knowing the punch wasn't the problem. He'd seen how hard Jack hit the deck and now he wondered if the old man would recall his charge on Vern.

"Leave him alone." Mary glared at her son. "Jack is not in any shape to be answering questions. Let's get him to the ship's doctor."

"I got this, Mom." Sam rushed to Jack's side and Justin followed. With one on each side, they gently lifted him to a standing position. Jack stumbled but seemed to be able to keep his balance. "Are you okay, Dad?"

Robert cringed at the word. "You're calling him Dad, now?"

"I guess I *am*." Sam turned to Jack and smiled. "He's more of Dad to me than our excuse for a father."

"I'm the first to admit our dad had his faults, but maybe he was just trying to make us better men. I know I deserved his punishment many times." Robert knew it was not that simple, but he wanted to believe he'd come from the seed of a good man.

"Neither of us deserved that kind of treatment and you of all people should know that. You got the belt far more often than I did—even when I'd done the dirty deed. I can't even count the number of times you saved my ass when we were kids."

Robert's voice softened. "You were such a puny little kid, Sam. I didn't think you'd survive."

"I probably wouldn't have, but now we have to make sure Jack survives Dad's evil hand. Won't you help me get him to the ship's doctor?"

Robert's voice turned cold again. "You and Justin can take him. I'm not so sure Jack's the innocent victim here. How do we know he didn't hit our dad? Maybe Dad's in worse shape." He turned his icy stare to Jack. "What do you say, Jack? Did you get a piece of my old man?"

Jack's eyes rolled back as his legs buckled. Justin and Sam held on, Sam scooping him into his arms and started to run toward the elevator by the stairs. "Come on Justin, let's get Jack to the doctor—quick." Mary followed them into the elevator, holding onto Jack's hand as they made their exit.

****

Robert poured a healthy shot of whiskey over the ice in the plastic tumbler. Cheap cabin couldn't even provide real glass—just a blue tinted plastic cup with white stenciled lettering advertising the cruise line, *Queen of the Seas*. God, he needed a drink. Unlike most people, a shot of Jack Daniels seemed to clear his mind rather than cloud his thinking. He drained the drink in his second swig just as a soft knock hit his door—a knock he'd been expecting.

He opened the door and pulled her in, planting a whiskey tainted kiss on her full, red lips. Darlene kicked the door shut with her three-inch spiked heel and wrapped her arms around Robert's neck. She didn't seem to mind the whiskey breath, even seemed to crave it as she pressed her body into his and deepened the kiss.

"Hold on, honey." Robert set his hands on her hips and pushed her away. "We've got some planning to do—

then we can get back to this." He patted her perfectly round ass—an ass so fine he hated to push it away.

"Oh, Bobby, you're always so serious." Her lips formed a perfect pout as she set her violet-blue eyes on his.

"One of us has to be." He shook her gaze and turned to make himself another drink. "Dad's little accident is going to change everything for us, but we gotta make sure things go our way."

"I know, baby, but we got this. Things worked out just right." With one quick pivot on her stiletto, she dropped her sweet behind on the bed and patted the spot beside her.

Robert accepted her invitation and joined her on the edge of the bed. "Yeah, Jack did us a big favor, all right. We just need to find a way to prove Jack pushed him over the edge."

"You're a witness, Bobby, isn't that enough?"

"Everyone knows I hate Jack. They'd never believe it coming from me. We need to get Jack to confess. Once his head clears, he'll remember what he did and we need to make sure he feels guilty enough to spills his guts."

"Do you think he'll confess?" Darlene put her hand on Robert's thigh, moving her shiny red nails toward her earlier target.

"Oh, yeah. He's such a stickler for the moral high ground, when his memory returns, he won't be able to stop himself from talking."

"But what if his head doesn't clear, Bobby? What if he doesn't remember things the way he should?" She tapped her stiff nail on his fly and he squirmed.

"Okay, baby, you got my attention." He swept her hand from his lap, holding it tight. "We'll just have to convince him he needs to tell the truth. With a little coercion, I think he'll remember." Guiding her hand back to its original destination, he leaned into her and wrapped his arms around his sweet Darlene. They'd done enough talking for tonight.

****

Waking up with Darlene's soft, warm body spooned into the curve of his limbs, Robert felt more alive than he'd felt in years. She was "the one"—the one he'd been waiting for since the day they met twenty-eight years ago, the day he started working for his dad. To be honest, he hadn't given her too much thought the first ten years; after all, she was a ten-year-old kid and he'd just graduated from high school when they met. There was no doubt she was a beautiful child, but he was an eighteen-year-old boy full of hormones—he had no time for little girls when there were eighteen-year-old women ready to tame Robert's desires. If his hormones hadn't led him into the arms of Suzanne Sizemore, a shapely blonde just waiting to fill her belly with Robert's child, things might have been different. He swore if he'd still been single when Darlene reached the age of consent, they would have gotten together twenty years ago.

But that's not how it worked out. Suzanne forgot to take her birth control pill and three kids later, Robert felt stuck in a loveless marriage. He'd probably still be there if his wife of twenty-five years hadn't run off with her yoga instructor, a woman who gave Suzanne the kind of love she hadn't been aware she was craving.

Robert had been furious, not because he loved Suzanne, but because she'd left him—a strong, virile man—for a woman. The fact that he was stuck with big alimony payments didn't help his mood in the least. He'd endured twenty agonizing years (the first five hadn't been so bad) just so he wouldn't have to give that bitch half of his hard-earned piece of the business. All those wasted years—years he could have been pursuing Darlene.

Throughout his entire twenty-five-year marriage, he'd kept Darlene in his sights. He really couldn't avoid seeing her since her mom, Gladys, worked for Bradley & Sons Construction. More accurately, Gladys Dunwoody ran Bradley & Sons and under her managerial authority the business grew and thrived. Watching his dad's uncharacteristic acquiescence when it came to Gladys was like watching a lion succumb to a seasoned lion tamer. Gladys definitely had him jumping through the proverbial hoop, which kept the business running smoothly. Robert often wondered if—and how—she rewarded him for his passive acceptance of her rigid rules.

Despite her no-nonsense approach, Robert liked Gladys—maybe because he got away with more than Vern for some reason. But what he liked most about Gladys was her daughter, Darlene, who often joined her mother at work and even helped out every summer to help pay for college. As the years passed Darlene transformed from a cute co-ed with a strawberry blonde ponytail and glasses into a breathtakingly beautiful woman. Whenever he saw her, his jeans felt a little tighter and his heart skipped a beat or two. He wanted her, but between his marriage and her popularity with numerous suitors, they never connected—not that he hadn't tried, but in spite of her open-minded attitude when it came to male companionship, she drew the line at married men in general and Robert in particular.

But three years ago, everything changed. Robert's divorce started him on the path to Darlene's door and while she continued to block his advances, he remained steadfast in his quest to win her heart. It didn't help that she'd been in a relationship with Eddie Bristowe for over five years—waiting for him to make his fortune with one of his fly-by-night schemes, after which they were planning to get married—at least that's what she told Robert. But Robert wasn't buying it and one day, Darlene quit buying Eddie's bullshit, too.

Darlene walked into work two years ago, her perfume announcing her arrival. With the scent of Obsession, she made a path straight to Robert's office. She closed the door, shut the blinds, and moved seductively around Robert's desk, planting her perfect ass on his lap. Until that day, they'd never kissed and when she took Robert's face in her soft manicured hands and leaned down to brush her full lips against his more severe, whisker covered mouth, the fireworks exploded. All the years of fantasizing about this woman seemed a black and white movie compared to the real thing. He finally had the woman of his dreams.

And now, two years later, he still couldn't get enough of Darlene Dunwoody and as he immersed his face into the thick blonde curls covering the pillow, he wondered how yesterday would change their lives.

Chapter Four

Wake Up

"Jack, wake up!" Mary's voice cracked as she shook her new husband's shoulder. "Please don't leave me. Open your eyes, damn it!"

"I'm tired, Mary. Just let me sleep." His voice was barely audible as he opened his eyes for his bride, but he just couldn't find the strength to speak any louder. "I'm so tired." Looking briefly at Mary, his eyelids fluttered and then snapped shut.

"Noooo." Mary shrieked. When his eyes popped open, she changed her tone to "loving wife mode"—Jack's favorite way of describing her normal, sweet style of speaking. As she touched his face, he inhaled the scent, Jergens lotion—a cherry-almond aroma that just said "Mary". "Please stay with me, honey. Open those big brown eyes so I can check your pupils again."

"Oh, Mary, I'm fine." Jack sat up, his voice louder now. "I'm tired because you keep waking me up. My vision is perfect, or it will be when I put on my glasses, and my brain is not damaged. The doctor said it was a mild concussion—mild, Mary. Mild!"

"If your brain is so damn good, why did you call me Nancy last time I woke you?"

"Because you woke me out of a pleasant sleep and started nagging me. That felt more like Nancy than you.

You've never spoken harshly to me, sweetie." He took her lotion scented hand from his forehead, pulled it down to his lap, and held it tight. "Never a harsh word in two years and the minute we're married it starts."

"I'm sorry, dear. I'm just so worried about you. What happened out there? Do you remember?"

"It's pretty foggy. Even a mild concussion can mess with your memory, I guess." Jack rubbed his forehead with his free hand. "I do remember Vern hitting me. But I got up and I was running toward him to take a swipe at him." His eyes stared straight ahead as he tried hard to conjure the memory. "I don't think I got the chance."

"Sorry to burst your bubble, dear, but I don't think you're a match for Vern. He's a big guy and even bigger now that his beer gut has expanded."

Visions of Vern's big gut flashed in Jack's mind—he wasn't sure why. "Hey, I may be small, but I'm tough. I've got game."

Mary laughed. "Yeah, you've got game all right. Your game is Trivial Pursuit. You're a genius and I love your brain, but physically I think Vern could take you." Her smile faded. "That bastard must have slammed you onto the deck then walked away. I wish I'd have gone after him last night. I'm so damn mad at him for ruining our wedding day."

"Please don't confront him. I don't want you putting yourself in danger." Jack kissed Mary softly and then slid back down onto his pillow. Mary followed his lead. "Besides, Vern could never ruin the feeling I felt when you said, 'I do'. Our wedding day will be a day we'll never forget and for some reason, I don't think Vern will be bothering us anymore."

"You're probably right. He'd better stay away after

what he did to you."

"Now can we go back to sleep? It's 3:00 a.m. and I hope you'll allow me the next four hours without waking me."

Mary sat up abruptly. "Oh, I almost forgot. Turn toward the light, dear. I need to check out your pupils."

Jack opened his eyes so wide he felt his face stretch. "Okay, take a look, then let's get some sleep. We dock at Puerto Vallarta at 8:00 a.m. and I'm going ashore."

"Are you sure you're up to it?"

"You bet your ass I am. I'm not coming all the way down here to sit on this damn ship." While Mary inspected his pupils, he studied her beautiful emerald-green eyes, feeling a love he'd never known before her. "I can't wait to share this adventure with you."

Mary leaned down and gently kissed his forehead. "I'm all in, dear. I'll set the alarm for 7:00 a.m. so we can get four straight hours of sleep."

Jack couldn't take his eyes off Mary as she rolled over to turn out the light. In the darkness, he reached out to pull her close. "I love you, sweetie."

"And I love you, Jack Madison—more than you'll ever know."

****

Justin stared at the flickering light bouncing off the ceiling. Was it the moonlight reflecting off the ocean or was it the sun on the rise, casting the bright image through his porthole? Or maybe the light of a passing ship—he had no idea what time it was or if he had dozed for a minute or an hour. He reached for his phone on the nightstand—5:00 a.m.—too early to get up, but too late to get much sleep. Visions of Grandpa Jack lying semi-conscious on the ship's deck kept swirling through his mind. He'd just gotten his grandpa back two years ago and the thought of losing him felt like a kick in the gut.

Annie rolled over and flopped her arm around Justin's waist. Reaching across, he caressed her soft skin while he continued to watch the light dance on the ceiling. "You awake, Annie?"

"I am now. You weren't exactly whispering."

Although he wasn't trying to wake her, his voice had a deep tone that was hard to keep low. And maybe he wasn't trying that hard to whisper. "Sorry, babe, I guess I was hoping you were awake."

"I wasn't sleeping that soundly anyway. Are you okay?" She moved her hand to his smooth chest.

"Not really. I'm so worried about Grandpa, and Mary, too. We need to go with them into town this morning."

"I'm with you on that. We need to stick very close to them. I don't think they have any idea how dangerous Vern might be."

"What makes you say that?" Justin asked. "I was just worried about his concussion. Do you think Vern's really going to cause more problems?"

Annie ran her left hand through her long dark hair, then propped herself on her right elbow. "I know that mentality. Mark my words, Vern is bad news."

"I don't doubt that he's trouble, but I think we can handle him. He's just a big bully." Justin rolled over to face Annie. "Let's make a pact to stick to Grandpa Jack and Mary like glue."

"Done." Annie brushed the lock of dark hair from Justin's forehead, then leaned in to kiss him. "I'm so lucky to have you in my life—we make a pretty good team."

"I'm the lucky one. I'm also the tired one, and I think I can finally fall asleep. Come closer, babe." He wrapped his arms around his girl, finally closed his eyes, and drifted off to sleep.

****

"Where are you going, sweet cheeks?" Robert's deep voice broke the silence of the still morning causing Darlene to trip over her lace panties, her "sweet cheeks" landing back on the bed in Robert's face.

"Is that all you think about is my ass? I have a brain you know."

"Of course, I don't just think about your ass; I love your beautiful brain," Robert lied. "Now where are you going in such a hurry?"

Reaching back, she ran her fingers through his mane of dark wavy hair. "I need to go say goodbye to Mom. I probably won't see her for a very long time."

"You can't blame her for getting the hell away from Seattle and starting a new life in Puerto Vallarta. Dad paid her well and now she can retire in peace." Maybe too well, Robert thought. Gladys put in thirty good years, but he wasn't sure she deserved the salary Vern paid her. Now she was going to live a better life than he was living.

"It might be nice for us, too, honey." Darlene caressed his cheek as she cooed the words.

"You know I can't leave the business right now. It's such a mess." How it had gone downhill so quickly he couldn't fathom.

Darlene winked at him. "It'll all be better soon." Her seductive violet-blue eyes held his gaze and as they silently connected, he knew she was right. Things would be better soon.

Darlene smelled of *Queen of the Seas* body wash, a

fresh citrus aroma that mixed well with the sea air. As she rose from the bed and finished dressing, every move was viewed through Robert's obsessed eyes. He would never get enough of her—never. Darlene was the love of his life, and he would not ever let her go. If she even thought of leaving, he was not above reminding her of all he'd done for her.

Robert was well aware of all her assets, but she had one serious liability—she couldn't balance the books. Gladys had done a marvelous job of managing the finances of Bradley & Sons, Inc., but she obviously hadn't passed the smart gene to her daughter. Darlene Dunwoody, better known in Robert's mind as Darlene Dumb-woody, was dumb as a rock and if it weren't for her perfectly shaped breasts and long legs, not to mention that fine ass, he would have fired her long ago. But brains weren't everything. His ex-wife had an IQ of 140 and that hadn't worked out so well. Yes, Darlene Dumb-woody was a perfect fit for Robert—he could be the smart one for a change. He liked the fact that she looked up to him, so for love and the best sex of his life, he could overlook a few accounting mistakes.

"Don't be too long. I'll be ready to get off this boat in about twenty minutes."

"Don't rush me, Robert. I'll be back when I'm good and ready." Darlene's tone didn't sit well with Robert.

"Well, I hope you're 'good and ready' in about thirty minutes." He wasn't going to let her get away with that snotty attitude, but he would give her ten more minutes. "I'll be waiting at the ramp."

The smile left Darlene's lips and her voice was flat. "Whatever you say, boss." She pulled on her high heels, grabbed her purse, and let herself out without turning back.

Chapter Five

Goodbye Gladys

Gladys answered the knock on her cabin door wearing the white fleece robe provided by *Queen of the Seas*.

"Darlene, honey, you're early." Gladys patted her wiry blonde hair; loose strands more gray than blonde, falling across her rimless glasses. Pulling the pins from her normally tight, topknot bun, her tresses fell to her shoulders.

"I'm not early. You should be ready to go. What's going on, Mom?" Darlene tried to lock onto her mother's blue eyes, but Gladys turned away. "Mom, what are you doing? Fix your hair and let's get out of here."

"My hair is fine. I don't need to be all neat and put together to live by myself in Mexico." Gladys dropped the robe and pulled on the yellow T-shirt and khaki shorts she'd laid out on the bed.

"What do you mean, by yourself? Where's Vern?" Darlene asked.

"He never showed up. Jack must have really pushed him over the edge." Gladys spoke in a monotone as she finished packing the last of her belongings.

"What? That can't be right. That wasn't the plan." Darlene's voice was shrill and her words came fast. "Robert said we were gonna fake his death, so you two could retire on half the insurance money and he could take the other half to salvage the business."

"Well, I suppose it's possible that Vern is just lying in a corner somewhere drunk, but even he wouldn't jeopardize this plan. If he were alive, he'd be here." Gladys positioned her sun hat over her uncharacteristically unkempt hair.

"Why aren't you more upset? I thought Vern was the love of your life?"

"Oh, God, no. I didn't mind being the other woman, but since Mary left him, he's been smothering me. Once a week was tolerable, but every night with that beer gut squishing the life out of me—no thanks."

"I really thought you loved him, Mom."

"I thought I did twenty-five years ago, when I was thirty-seven and struggling. I needed someone to help me with the bills after your no-good father left us and, I gotta admit, Vern and I matched up pretty well in the sack back then." Gladys finally smiled and turned her gaze to her daughter. "He was always real sweet to me—he knew better than to cross me—I think he knew I'd hit back. His slaps and slugs were saved for Mary and his boys. But now that Mary's gone, he's itching to use that big fat fist of his on a new target, and I'm next in line." She rubbed her thigh, revealing a blue and yellow bruise likely planted in the last week. "As you can see, he's already made his mark, although I don't think he intended to grab me so hard."

"Why didn't you say anything? Jesus, Mom, you don't need that."

"Yeah, I know. I've been able to control him so far, but when he didn't show up last night, I gotta say I wasn't that sorry." Darlene noticed Gladys' body heave, maybe

43

with a sigh of relief. Her voice seemed shaky as she continued. "So, Robert confirmed that Vern was alive after the fight with Jack?"

"Well, not in so many words. I know that was the plan, but he didn't actually say Vern was alive." The color drained from Darlene's normally tanned face. "Oh my God! Do you think Robert finished the job Jack started? Am I sleeping with a killer?"

"Robert wouldn't hurt Vern, would he?" Gladys seemed momentarily concerned. "Robert is the only one in that family who seemed to like Vern—always sticking up for him when Sam or Mary said anything negative."

Darlene cringed at her mother's use of the past tense—"seemed to like him"—acting like he was dead. She kept that observation to herself. "If you ask me, Robert's loyalty is an act. He may think he deserved the treatment he got from his dad, but deep down I think he really hates Vern. Sometimes he gets so angry when I ask him about his childhood, I think he's gonna have a stroke or something."

Gladys finished shoving the last of her belongings into her overnight bag. "Well, I think we should stick to the story that Jack did it. Robert shouldn't have to pay for killing that son of a bitch." Pulling up the handle to her rolling bag, she seemed ready to leave the ship for her new life. "Let me know when the life insurance gets paid. I still want my half—Vern or no Vern."

"Mom, are you going to be okay? Do you have enough money for now?" Darlene had never spent a day without her mom or a man, so she didn't understand her mother's ability to live alone in a new environment. She hugged Gladys and got a light pat in return.

"Oh, hell, yes. I've skimmed enough off the top of

those books over the past twenty-five years to make a nice life for myself. I don't need the life insurance, but don't tell Robert. I could use a bigger condo down here."

"Oh, okay." Darlene's stomach was churning with anxiety. Her heart skipped a beat as she grabbed and clung to her mom's hand. "Aren't you a little upset about Vern, though? Money is one thing, but murder…?"

"Oh, for all we know, he's just drunk. He'll probably show up at the condo, but honestly, I hope he doesn't." Her face devoid of expression, Gladys stared into her daughter's eyes. "We would all be better off without Vern."

"I guess so…"

Gladys pulled her hand from Darlene's grip and headed for the door. "Hey, honey. Could you do me a favor and wait here for them to pick up my trunk? They should be here by 8:30."

"Okay, but why didn't you just have this stuff shipped."

"My life is in that trunk—all my most precious possessions. I wanted to keep it close. Can't you just do this for me?" Gladys said with the tone that always made Darlene feel guilty, even when she'd done nothing wrong.

"Sure, Mom." A lump rose in Darlene's throat and tears threatened to sabotage her cool image. "It's just that, I don't want to be alone right now. I'm losing you and Robert may be a killer and, shit, I don't know what to think." Her hands were shaking now as the tears broke loose.

Gladys dropped her bag, turned to her daughter, grabbed her firmly by the shoulders, and shook her—as she had so often throughout Darlene's childhood. "Snap

45

out of it! Don't be a God damn crybaby and don't blow this for all of us. We're looking at five million bucks thanks to Vern." She loosened her grip and reached for her bag. "I need to get going before anyone recognizes me. I don't need Mary asking any questions."

With a deep breath, Darlene tried to cover the fear she felt with a strong steady voice. "Bye, Mom. Have a nice life down here. I love you." She grabbed her mother in a final hug.

"Don't be so needy. I'm not dying, just moving. We'll talk soon." Gladys removed herself from Darlene's embrace, opened the door, and walked out.

****

Would things ever change with her mom? Darlene sat silently staring at the door that had just shut her mother out of her life—probably forever. Her eyes drifted from the door to the trunk, wondering what keepsakes her mother couldn't live without. Gladys had never been sentimental, as evidenced by the lack of even one school project from Darlene's youth in her childhood home. Other moms plastered their children's poems and drawings to every spare spot on the refrigerator, but the Dunwoody fridge was shiny and spotless. Gladys just wasn't the warm, fuzzy type—at least not after her cheating husband, Calvin, cleaned out their bank account and ran off with Darlene's babysitter. As Darlene grew older, she often wondered if her mom blamed her for the demise of her marriage; after all, without Darlene, there would have been no need for a babysitter to tempt Calvin.

After Calvin left, Gladys turned a cold eye to the world in general and to Darlene specifically. She provided the basics to her little girl, but her words were harsh, and her love was conditional at best—that is, until she met Vern. At the age of ten, Darlene had been without a father for five years and as Vern tried to impress Gladys, he showered little Darlene with dolls, trinkets, and games. At the time, Darlene didn't understand why she was sent to her room, with the door locked, as soon as the items touched her hand; she was just grateful for the attention, no matter how brief, from Vern and even a few kind words and gentle pats from her mom. She equated her mother's touch as well as the gifts with love, but it was not love for her. As the years passed, she understood the love was all for Gladys as evidenced by the sound of squeaking bedsprings that followed each offering.

Now as Darlene waited for the men to retrieve Gladys' trunk, she wondered if her mother had ever loved her. She also wondered what was in the trunk. What could be so important to a woman who didn't have a sentimental bone in her body? No, this didn't make sense. She marched her stilettos across the room—it was only 8:15—she had time to check it out before the men arrived. Reaching for the latch, she hesitated. Should she look at her mother's private stash? The decision was seemingly clear as she found the case was locked, but then she remembered a trick with a hairpin—her mother had taught her well—and the lock was released. Opening the lid, she couldn't believe her eyes. She gasped as a knock interrupted her thoughts. After snatching one small item from the trunk, she slammed the lid closed, took a deep breath, walked slowly across the cabin, and opened the door.

Chapter Six

Going Ashore

"Are you sure you're up for this, Grandpa?" Justin reached for Jack's hand as they headed down the steep ramp.

Jack didn't want to admit he was feeling a little dizzy and considered pushing Justin away, but he took the helping hand. "I'm fine, but if you really want to hold your grandpa's hand, I won't stop you." He laughed, trying to make light of his infirmity. "Come on Mary, Annie—we should all hold onto each other."

Mary took her place on Jack's left side, lacing her fingers through his and using her other hand to hold his arm. Annie completed the foursome by hugging the rail and leaning into Justin. Then as they were about to step off the ramp…

"Watch out!" A voice behind them screamed. "Get out of the way! Now!"

Jack turned in time to see a huge trunk strapped to a dolly, careening toward Mary. He pulled her toward him as Justin hauled them both around the rail and onto the dock. They fell in a pile, Jack's head colliding with Justin's younger, harder head.

"Not again." Jack rubbed his forehead. "This headache is never going to go away at this rate."

Justin shook his head. "Tell me about it. What the

fuck just happened?"

Their eyes turned toward the big black metal trunk lying less than ten feet from them. A small gray head peeked over the top.

"My god, Aunt Dot, are you okay?" Justin jumped up to check on his great aunt.

Pushing herself up by leaning on the trunk, Aunt Dot stood and shook her ankle. "Just a bruise, I think. I almost made it clear, but I didn't get my foot out of the way in time."

"What are you doing down here all alone?" Justin asked.

"Don't you go worrying about me. I may be old, but I can take care of myself." Her voice was strong and sharp for an eighty-five-year-old woman. "I woke up early and thought I'd wait for Sam and Jamie down here. It's such a beautiful day and what a perfectly marvelous place for people watching."

Jack rose, rubbing his head. "Don't worry about her. She's tougher than you and I put together. It will take more than a runaway trunk to take this woman down."

"Don't I know it. She's been kicking my ass since the day I was born," Justin said. "If it weren't for her, my mom and I probably wouldn't have made it through my first few years."

Jack silently thanked his Aunt Dot every day for being there for his daughter, Jamie, twenty-six years ago. Still trying to forgive himself for not being with her through her teenage pregnancy, Jack felt lucky to have Jamie and his grandson, Justin, back in his life. He had failed them so many years ago, but when he dropped the ball, fate had stepped in by passing the ball to Aunt Dorothy who had been living a short bus ride away from

Jamie's place of exile, Berkeley, California.

"Are you sure you're okay, Dot?" Jack asked. "Maybe we should have you checked out."

"I think I'm going to get checked out whether I want to or not." She looked up the ramp as a starched white uniform wrapped around a frantic officer came running down the ramp. The two workmen who were supposed to be controlling the trunk followed with tentative steps.

"Folks, I'm sorry for the disruption. We have a passenger trying to get some precious cargo off the ship and these two gentlemen were trying to handle it most carefully. It seems they lost their hold, but everyone seems fine here, right?" He put his hand on Aunt Dot's shoulder. "Let me buy you lunch in Puerto Vallarta—for you and all your friends over here." He handed vouchers to each person for a waterfront restaurant. "And when you come back, please come to my office to sign the incident report."

Jack's head was throbbing. "Do we still get lunch if we don't sign off on your report?"

"Of course. Of course. No pressure. We want to be sure you're all right. Did this thing hit anyone?"

"I think it swiped my Aunt Dorothy's ankle. We jumped out of the way, but Jack and I cracked skulls in our attempt to get out of the way." Justin rolled his head slowly and rubbed his temple.

"Well, we're happy to have our doctors check you out."

"Thanks, but can it wait till we get back this evening? We don't want to spend our only day in this port having our heads examined," Justin said.

"So, you must be just fine if you can spend a day ashore." Was this guy trying to guilt them into signing off on the accident?

Jack spoke up. "As of now, I have a concussion from slipping on your deck last night and maybe another head injury from avoiding some passenger's trunk. But I'll be damned if I'll let you stop me from enjoying my honeymoon." Reaching for Mary's hand and motioning to Justin and Annie, he took a step away from the officer, then turned back. "We'll let you know if we need medical attention as soon as we get back from our free lunch."

Aunt Dot smiled. "Ditto. We'll let you know. But, in the meantime, could you give me a couple more lunch vouchers for my niece and her husband?"

"Sure. No problem." He handed her two more vouchers.

As Officer Rodriguez walked away, the two bumbling workmen with the slippery fingers, set about righting the dolly and re-attaching the bungee cords around the trunk. The lock had broken, and the lid threatened to swing open as they lifted what appeared to be a very heavy case. What the hell was in that thing? Pushing the lid down and clicking the lock in place, the men juggled and steadied the trunk, then pushed it off the dock toward a waiting van.

Annie attached herself to Justin, hugging him so tight he gasped for air. "Whoa, baby. We just survived a runaway trunk. Don't squeeze the life out of me."

"Sorry, Justie, I'm just so glad we made it off the ramp. We could have all been killed."

Mary moved to Jack, holding his face in her hands and kissing him gently. "We're all still alive. Just smell that ocean air and have you ever seen a bluer sky? We have a lot to be thankful for, so let's put this behind us and enjoy our day."

Jack wrapped his arms around his woman. "I'm ready to enjoy this day and all the rest of our days, dear." He pulled back and took her hand, then turned to Aunt Dot. "Do you want us to wait here with you or do you just want to meet us at the restaurant at noon?"

"I think I'll be safe here now. I can't imagine any more trunks falling down the ramp." She waved her hand at the four of them. "You go on and have fun."

****

Aunt Dot watched as the workmen struggled to load the trunk into their van. It looked like a pretty shabby excuse for a vehicle, but being in Mexico, maybe the options for moving had a more local flavor. Not her problem, but whoever wanted their precious cargo moved might have chosen someone besides these two buffoons.

She turned her attention back to the ramp and all the colorful characters disembarking. A young couple caught her attention, kissing every few steps— obviously, newlyweds—the girl's yellow flowered skirt swaying with each inviting step. Dot figured they'd be back in their cabin by noon. Behind them an attractive older woman with long black hair pushed a wheelchair down the ramp. She struggled to guide the chair holding what appeared to be a large woman in a ruffled red skirt and a shawl that looked more like a bedcover than wrap. Completing the obvious sun cover, the woman wore a large floppy hat, oversized sunglasses, and a scarf over her face. Why the hell was this woman bothering to venture outside when she appeared averse to the sun? People were, indeed, funny.

And, strange. Dot looked up past the wheelchair and

there, at 8:45 in the morning, was a woman in a black cocktail dress and stilettos, screaming. "Stop that van!" Even in heels, she maneuvered the ramp with a quick step reaching the dock as the van's tires screeched and pulled away from the curb. Dropping to her knees only a few feet away from Dot, she bowed her head, clutched a letter to her chest, and whispered, "Damn it."

Chapter Seven

Darlene's Dilemma

"Are you okay, lady?" Dot stooped down to put her arm around the woman in the black cocktail dress.

Darlene flinched at the sensation of the old woman's rough, gnarly hand on her bare shoulder, quickly turning to see if she was in danger. Seeing that the hand belonged to a harmless little lady, she let out a gasp, or perhaps a sigh of relief, then stammered. "I-I guess so. I mean, No. I'm not okay. I'm not even close to okay, damn it!" Her voice was getting louder—she felt like she was about to explode. What the hell, she'd never see this sweet old woman again and she needed to dump her emotional load. "I think my mom may have done something horrible and I just let those two guys dispose of the evidence."

"Why would you think that, dear?" Dot kept her soft, dark eyes on Darlene, giving Darlene every reason to believe she was kind and sympathetic.

Darlene wanted to get this off her chest, but maybe she should keep her mouth shut. Wiping tears in the corners of her eyes that threatened to roll down her cheeks, she took a deep breath of warm, salty sea air. "I think I may be overreacting. My mom isn't the warm and fuzzy type and I think I may be reading more into this than I should. I'm sure everything will be fine."

"What did you think she'd done?" Dot asked, trying hard not to appear nosy.

"It's too crazy to believe. I thought she might have…"

"Darlene!" Robert's voice bellowed from behind her.

Darlene jumped to her feet. "Robert, what are you doing here?"

"I might ask you the same. We were supposed to meet at the top of the ramp right about now, but I see you haven't even changed your clothes. What's going on?" Looking up, Darlene cowered under his six-foot-two presence. The cool blue steel blazing from his eyes told her she was out of favor.

"I'm sorry. I was just talking to this nice lady about my mom."

"I don't think this 'nice lady' needs to know our business. Now, go change your clothes," Robert said in a hushed but terse tone.

"But I need to tell you something and I think I need to tell you now. We need to track down my mom."

Robert yanked her away from Dot, out of earshot. "What do you mean, track her down? Don't you know where she went?"

"I never got her address. Did you get it from your dad?"

"That's your job, honey. You're my secretary. You're supposed to handle all that shit. I can't believe you don't know where she is."

"I have her cell phone number. I can call her, but she hasn't answered so far."

"Why do you need to talk to her, anyway? She's retired and moved on and maybe we won't have to share the life insurance money if we can't find them. Maybe we should quit answering our phones."

"But I think your dad might actually be dead and I'm pretty sure my mom killed him—or is going to kill him." Darlene looked over her shoulder to see the old lady inching closer to them. Had she heard their conversation?

Robert appeared to be oblivious to the surroundings and spoke a little too loudly. "That's impossible!"

"Impossible?" Darlene lowered her voice as she took Robert's hand and pulled him farther from nosy ears. "Why would you say that? Have you seen Vern? Do you know if he's alive?"

"Of course, he's not alive. I saw Jack push him over the edge." Robert's words were louder than necessary. Was he hoping to be heard?

"You told me he didn't go over the edge."

"Well, now I'm telling you he did. I saw it. Jack Madison killed my father."

"Robert, what are you saying? This was supposed to be a faked death so we could get the money." Darlene had a sinking feeling in her stomach. Something wasn't adding up. "Were you lying to me last night?"

Robert grabbed her wrist, a little too hard she thought. Dragging her up the ramp, passengers stared as he controlled her movement. "C'mon, Darlene, let's get back to my cabin where we can discuss this in private."

****

Watching the man pull the young woman past her, Dot wondered if she should intervene. "Hey!" she yelled.

"Hey, Aunt Dot!" Jamie answered. She and Sam were coming down the ramp with little Rosie in tow. They stopped when they saw Robert, Sam sharing a few words with his brother and Darlene. Robert's grip seemed to loosen, and Darlene smiled. Dot didn't really know Robert, but if he was Sam's brother, she thought he was probably okay. She waited at the bottom of the ramp for Jamie and Sam to join her.

"So, have you been people watching while you waited for us?" Jamie asked. "Anything interesting?"

"You wouldn't believe me if I told you." Dot rubbed her ankle and leaned in to hug Jamie, then Sam. "Let me at that little girl of yours." Rosie was settled into Sam's baby backpack and as Sam bent his knees to bring her down to Dot's level, Dot pinched the little girl's cheek, evoking a spirited giggle. The drama of the last twenty minutes faded as Dot inhaled the sweet smell of baby lotion and a lingering whiff of bananas as Rosie let out an unladylike belch.

Jamie reached for Dot's familiar hand. Dot knew Jamie thought of her more like a mom than a great-aunt. And why wouldn't she—her own mother, Nancy, abandoned her through her teenage pregnancy. If Jamie had listened to her mother, Justin would never have been born and who knows what she would have thought of her second pregnancy twenty-five years later—she likely would have told her to remove that fetus, too, this time because she was too old—over forty, for God's sake.

"You produce the sweetest kids—even if they are twenty-five years apart." Dot said with a smile.

"Well, I've got one of each now, so I think I'll call it quits." Jamie laughed.

Sam chimed in. "Oh yeah. We're done. This little one keeps us busy, and we aren't getting any younger."

"By the way," Dot said, "We're meeting your dad and Justin—and Mary and Annie, of course—for lunch at this Oceanside restaurant." She flashed the coupons.

"How did you score those?" Jamie asked.

"It's a long story. I'll give you all the gory details on our way into town. It's been an interesting morning, to say the least."

****

Robert pulled Darlene down the long hallway to his cabin, his grip tightening with each step. No words were exchanged, leaving Darlene to ponder her fate. What if Robert killed Vern? Would he kill her, too? No one had ever accused her of critical thinking, so hopefully Robert would think she was too dumb to figure things out. Despite evidence to the contrary, she was nearly a genius with an IQ of 152, but she'd made a decision long ago to keep that information to herself. That hadn't been her original plan, but in college she found her brains weren't nearly as effective as her vacant smile and her beautifully shaped ass. Now she needed all her brainpower to figure out how to approach Robert.

"Hey, Bobby, calm down." She pulled her wrist free as Robert opened the cabin door.

"I can't calm down while you're sharing our secrets with Jack's aunt." He turned away and headed for the whiskey, pouring a healthy shot into the blue plastic cup. "We can't jeopardize our plan."

"Oh, God, I didn't know that old lady was Jack's aunt. But I think there might be a change in plans. See this?" She waved the envelope she'd been holding in front of Robert's face.

"Yeah, so what is it?" Robert pushed her hand away.

"It's a suicide note from you father." She unfolded the note she'd retrieved from the plain white envelope. The college ruled notebook paper seemed an odd choice for a suicide note, but that would be consistent with Vern's character—or lack of it.

"That's not possible. My dad would never kill himself."

"This note says otherwise. It says he can't live with himself anymore after all the pain he's caused the people he loves."

"Now I know that's not my dad. I don't think he had any idea he caused us pain. He thought everything he did was for our own good." Darlene watched Robert's head droop, his eyes glued to the floor. He spoke softly. "I can't believe Dad would do this."

Darlene moved closer to Robert, took the whiskey from his hand, and lifted his chin, forcing him to look into her eyes. "Here's the note. It looks like your dad's handwriting."

Robert took the note and examined the words. A tear looked like it was forming in his normally cold blue eyes, then he blinked. "Wait. How did you get this? Isn't this the kind of note you find by someone's dead body?"

"I found this in Mom's trunk. It looks like Vern's handwriting, but I'm ninety-nine percent sure my mom wrote this note. She forged so many documents and signatures over her years with your dad, she knew every curve of his cursive scrawl. But I know the difference."

"I thought she loved my dad. Do you think she'd really kill him?" Robert said.

"If someone didn't beat her to it. Maybe that's why she still has the note."

"Why would you think someone beat her to it?" Robert turned away again and reached for the whiskey. This time he didn't let Darlene deter him from the golden liquid and poured it down his throat in one swig.

"Because when I talked to her an hour ago, she hadn't seen Vern all night. She didn't seem that upset about it—said she hoped he'd really fallen overboard. Maybe she'd already killed him and just forgot to leave the note." Darlene was thinking too much and probably saying too much—would Robert figure out she had a brain? She continued anyway. "I know Mom didn't expect me to find this note and, to be honest, I wasn't planning to look in her trunk. That's not like me, but her strange behavior made me curious."

"Did you find anything else?"

"Nothing that important. It was weird, though, all my old class photos were there and all my artwork that never made it to the front of the refrigerator. I'd assumed she threw all that away." Darlene put her arms around Robert and laid her head on his chest, her voice trailed off. "She never acted like she cared about that stuff when I was growing up."

"Are you okay, honey?" Robert rubbed her back softly and somewhat uncharacteristically. He was usually all about the sex, but this felt like he really cared.

She lifted her head. "Not really. First, I find out my mom actually cared about me and then I find out she's capable of murder. I wanted to dig deeper in that trunk to see if there was something I was missing, but the moving guys knocked on the door before I had a chance to go further. I just grabbed the envelope, snapped the lock shut, and opened the door." Loosening her grip on Robert, she pulled her arms forward and pounded his chest. "I shouldn't have let them take the trunk and now I'll never know."

"Oh, don't worry, Gladys is going to let us find her. She needs to give us an address to send the insurance money. She's probably just waiting until the ship leaves, but we can come back—and we will." Robert obviously felt the courage of the whiskey. "My dad may be a son of a bitch, but I'll be damned if I'm gonna let your mom get away with murder. He has to die on my terms, at Jack's hand."

"Whatever you say, Bobby." Darlene felt guilty. Robert and Vern had cooked up this scheme because they needed the insurance money to keep the business going. But, if her mom hadn't embezzled so much and if Mom hadn't taught Darlene how to do the same, the company would be solvent. A pang of regret passed through Darlene's heart, but then it was gone. Soon she would have five million remedies to cure her guilt and regret.

Chapter Eight

Puerto Vallarta

Gladys leaned on the railing of her terrace, then swayed backward. Her new home, a condo just north of the Marina, was on the fifth floor—a relatively short fall to the beach below considering the building had twenty floors, but just as deadly a distance. Fear of heights had not been on her radar until she stood staring at the sea from this lofty perch, but suddenly she felt dizzy. Thick, salty air stung her nostrils and lay heavily on her chest as she dropped into the soft, white-cushioned lounge chair. Eighty-eight degrees with seventy percent humidity had her re-thinking her retirement decision, not only for the discomfort in her lungs, but for the frizzy hair days that would plague her from June through September.

The tri-tone ding of her cell phone sounded in her pocket. Pulling it out to look, she was not surprised to see it was Darlene again. She wasn't ready to talk to her yet—Darlene had too many questions and Gladys had too few answers to satisfy her inquisitive daughter. I'll call her tomorrow, she thought, after the ship has sailed.

As independent as Gladys viewed herself, this move had her feeling surprisingly uncomfortable, a sign of weakness she had never shown Darlene—a vulnerability she was not about to reveal now. The events of the past few days had left her physically bruised by a man she'd once loved and emotionally drained by the only logical conclusion she was able to reach—Vern was dead. There was no doubt Vern could be a real asshole and although her first thought was relief that he would not be joining her, she now felt the tiniest stab of regret. Rubbing the bruise on her thigh, she had to admit it had not come out of violence, but from his vise-like grip as she straddled him in one last goodbye fuck. He'd clearly enjoyed it, commenting on her renewed enthusiasm for his lovemaking. The fact that he hadn't felt the need to dominate with the usual missionary position made the ride much more pleasant for Gladys as she took the top and navigated around his ever-growing gut. She couldn't remember the last time they'd matched up so well, but the memory of the warm afterglow would have to hold her—she was getting a little old to attract a new Sugar Daddy and she sure as hell wasn't looking for love. Vern was gone and now she would be alone with only her money to keep her company…and soon there would be a couple million more dollars. She could live with that.

****

Jack knew Justin and Annie would have preferred a walk along the beach toward town, an easy couple of miles for twenty-somethings and normally doable for healthy senior citizens, but Jack wasn't ready for the trek.

"I'm sorry, guys. I wish I could make the hike, but in this heat—and with this headache—I need to take a taxi." Jack leaned into Mary, holding her hand as tightly as a drowning man holding a lifeline.

"It's fine with me, dear." Mary wiggled her fingers prompting Jack to loosen his vise-like grip. With her now more mobile fingers, she squeezed his hand, then turned to their younger companions. "Do you two want to meet us in town?"

"No way." Justin said. "We want to ride with you newlyweds and enjoy the glow of young love." As he said the words, Annie smiled and held her hands up in a "heart" shape.

Jack laughed. "I know you're playing loose with the term 'young', but just wait till you get to this age. I still think of myself as young. Sixty-nine doesn't feel that much different than twenty-nine, that is, unless you face plant on the ship's deck."

"Sorry, Grandpa. I didn't mean to underestimate either of you. Maybe you'll want to join my softball league."

"You're God damn right I want to join your league. Too bad I don't live closer." He winked at Justin. Jack was a damn good player in his day but, luckily, he wouldn't have to prove it. Feeling young was one thing, but maybe he wasn't quite as athletic as his twenty-six-year-old grandson.

"So, let's grab that cab." Justin said as he waved down the taxi heading for the curb.

****

Age certainly wasn't an issue with Aunt Dot. "Come on, Jamie, Sam. You walk about as slow as a herd of elephants." Continuing her breakneck pace, she looked back over her shoulder.

Jamie stomped her foot. "No, you slow down. There's a lot to see here and we're hauling an eighteen-month-old. What's the big hurry?"

Stopping reluctantly, Dot said. "Hey, I'm eighty-five years old. My time could be up tomorrow. I want to squeeze everything into the time I have left on this planet." So far, she'd squeezed in two husbands and twenty-five-year lover. The two husbands hadn't worked out so well, but Irving was everything the other two were not. Even so, she decided not to marry her lover, choosing to live in sin long before it was fashionable for a woman of her age. "I'm not going to keep waiting to enjoy my life like Irving. He always thought he'd do things tomorrow and look what happened to him." Irving had, in fact, been hit by a tour bus as he crossed the street—he was heading to a travel agency to finally book his dream trip to Europe. He'd been gone two years now.

Jamie put her arm around Aunt Dot. "I remember the day you met Irving. I feel joyfully responsible for your meeting. If you hadn't met me outside the door of my European History class, you never would have met Professor Blumenfeld."

Dot leaned into Jamie, smiling through her tears. "That would have been the best day of my life if it hadn't been followed by twenty-five years of almost perfect days."

"Almost perfect?" Jamie laughed.

"Well, I would have liked to take that trip to Europe with him and I gave him shit about being a homebody. I'd give anything for another twenty-five years at home with Irving over any trip." Dot wiped her eyes. "But he's gone now and I'm going to enjoy what's left of my life— every single moment."

Jamie knew all too well about living for the moment. Although she was deeply in love with Sam, she still saved a piece of her heart for her first husband, Paul— his loss seven years ago as painful as it was unexpected. Aunt Dot was right, they needed to make the most of each day. Jamie reached for Dot's hand and caught her misty eye. "Okay, we'll try to keep up with you. There's lots to see before we reach the restaurant."

****

Jack was tired, but he'd made it through the cobblestone streets of old Puerto Vallarta with only a few short respites. What a lucky man he was to have Mary by his side on this journey—the journey that would take them both another twenty or maybe even thirty years into the future. Time to see little Rosie grow up and time to see Justin and Annie marry and have children of their own.

But now it was time for lunch, although a free meal was little consolation for a concussion and a new head wound from that God damn trunk incident. He could feel the new bruise forming on his forehead. Did Justin feel the same dizzy sensation from the blow or was it the double whack that was causing Jack to stagger. He could make it two more blocks, couldn't he? Food and hopefully an air-conditioned room was just what he needed.

"Come on, dear, we're almost there." Mary held Jack's arm, guiding them toward their destination.

Justin's furrowed brow and somber half-smile sent a message to Jack that he probably looked like shit. "Nice day in town today, huh, Grandpa?" Justin's voice was a little too perky in Jack's opinion. Now he knew he looked like death warmed over—exactly how he felt but he couldn't ruin his family's day.

"Yeah, yeah. Lots of trinkets and fancy churches. I've had enough of that. I'm ready to eat," Jack lied. He really loved the stained-glass opulence of the cathedral, and he was a sucker for sentimental keepsakes, calling it crap out loud, but displaying every piece of crap proudly after each adventure. Before Mary, he'd rarely ventured beyond his backyard, but once they met, they hit the road, acquiring their share of logo golf balls, refrigerator magnets, and knick-knacks from their escapades. Now he wasn't thinking of keepsakes. He just wanted to sit down.

"Here we are, dear. And there's Jamie, Sam, Dot, and our little Rosie." She led Jack to the table, where the aroma of jalapeno peppers and spicy beef invaded his nostrils.

Jamie stood to hug her dad, her smile fading as she stretched her arms toward him. As Jack opened his arms to meet Jamie's embrace, he collapsed.

****

"Let's go to your dad's cabin to see what's going on." Darlene pleaded her case, but Robert didn't respond. "Don't you want to know what happened to your dad?"

"I don't know. My dad can be a real son-of-a-bitch, but I'm not sure I'm ready to face his death." He poured another shot of whiskey into the blue plastic cup, took a deep breath inhaling the intoxicating scent, then sent it down his throat. "He's not so bad now that Mom's gone, and Sam and I are grown. It wasn't easy growing up with him, but I don't want him to die—I really don't want him to die. Is that weird?"

"No, it's not weird. I think you and I are a lot alike. We keep making excuses for our shitty parents, hoping we'll get their love and approval. And for some reason, we still love them."

"Why? Why do I still give a shit? Screw it, let's go to his cabin and see what's going on. I have his extra key. He's just a few doors down." Robert put his arm around

Darlene and led her to the door and down the corridor.

With no response to their knocking, they used the key to enter the room. It smelled of Vern's cologne and stale whiskey with no sign of Vern himself. The bed looked like it had been slept in with the sheets thrown back and the pillows bearing the greasy mark of Vern's hair pomade. But there was something missing. The red bedspread was not on the bed, or the floor or anywhere in the room.

"Oh my God, my mom did kill Vern." Darlene grabbed Robert's arm as they stood at the end of the bed.

"Why do you say that?"

"When I opened Mom's trunk, there was something red under the pictures. She must have wrapped Vern in the red bedspread and shoved him in her trunk."

Robert's knees buckled and he fell to the floor. "No, this can't be happening. This was not the plan." Robert hadn't shed a tear in years, but now he put his head in his hands and cried as Darlene knelt beside him.

****

Gladys had barely settled into the lounge chair on the deck when the doorbell rang. Her trunk had arrived— no one else but Vern had her address, so she assumed her most precious keepsakes were about to be wheeled into her condo.

She opened the door to two big, hairy guys in white sleeveless T-shirts. "We got your trunk, lady, but we need another hundred bucks to take it off this dolly."

"That wasn't our arrangement. You already got your money."

"Lady, we didn't know how heavy this thing was gonna be. It feels like there's a dead body in here. Plus, the latch broke and we had to wrap a bungee cord around it. It was a pain in the ass, and we want more money."

"Fine." Gladys didn't want any trouble from these guys. They didn't look like anyone she wanted to challenge. She got her purse and gave them another hundred dollars. "Just set it in the dining room."

They let it down with a thud. "It's all yours, lady."

Gladys shut the door behind them, glad to have her trunk safe and secure. She walked slowly toward the black box, knelt beside it, and lifted the broken latch. Pushing the pictures on top aside, she reached in for the red tablecloth covering the precious cargo. She took the red table covering—her favorite from her own childhood—and spread it on her new table.

Chapter Nine

Is Everyone All Right?

"I can't take you anywhere." Mary hoped her pissed off voice covered her fear. Jack was going to survive this concussion, but he was giving her a hell of a scare.

Jack was smiling now, even as his new bride spewed the harsh words. "Well, you're stuck with me now, sweetie. Didn't know what you signed on for, did you?"

"Well, it just so happens I'm happy to be stuck with you." She returned his smart-ass smile, trying to make light of the situation, but inside she was fuming. "If it weren't for Vern, you'd be fine. That son of a bitch just can't stop interfering in my life." This was the final straw; she was determined to confront Vern. He'd done plenty of damage to her and her boys when they were married—now he was messing with her new husband. He had to be stopped!

Jack looked up at her and all the faces hovering above him. "Show's over. Let's get some food. Don't want to waste those coupons."

An hour had passed since Jack had collapsed and the emergency medical team had been called. After tests and monitoring, the paramedics assured Mary he just needed more hydration, food, and rest. Tonight, she should let him sleep without waking him every hour to check his pupils—his exhaustion was more pronounced than his concussion, but the combination was just too much for him on this hot afternoon. They'd pumped him full of liquid, while reminding him to make sure he downed eight glasses of water. Now, as they removed the IV, he had another problem.

"Okay, I've been rehydrated. Now I gotta pee!" He jumped to his feet, swaying a little.

"Me, too." Justin said as he took Jack's arm to steady him. "Let's go. The rest of you get back to your margaritas and we'll be right back."

"Are you sure you want to eat?" Mary asked Jack.

"You're God damn right I want to eat. Even when I was unconscious, the smell of those burritos found their way up my nose. I swear that's what woke me up. I'm so hungry I wish I had two coupons."

Mary watched her husband and his grandson walk away, arm in arm, happy to see Jack back to his old, wise-cracking self, even if a bit unsteady. The rest of the family seemed to breathe a collective sigh of relief as Jack moved tentatively toward the restroom.

Aunt Dot called after him, "Don't lollygag in there. We're all hungry."

Dot, Jamie, Sam, and Rosie took one side of the long table, while Mary sat with Annie on the other side waiting for their men to return. The huge bay window allowed them to look out at the ocean where seagulls were flying low, looking for their next meal. If it weren't for Jack, they might be out on the deck, inhaling the salt air, but under the circumstances, air conditioning inside seemed the right choice.

Mary looked around at her new family. She and her son, Sam, fit so well with the Madison crew. It seemed odd that Sam had developed into a loving, compassionate man while his brother, Robert found nothing but cynicism in his world. Hopefully, Robert would come around and join this family someday.

Damn Vern! He was the cause of this discord. He'd be sorry he hurt her husband—she'd see to that as soon as she got back to the ship. Tonight, she would let Jack rest while she went to pay a visit to Vern.

****

"This isn't right, Bobby. If Mom wanted this to look like a suicide, where's Vern's body?" Darlene picked up the pill bottle—Ambien. "Mix this with whiskey and he damn sure isn't feeling well if he's not dead."

"I still can't believe he might actually be dead. But he must be, I mean, if he were alive wouldn't he have taken his favorite shirt?" Robert stared at the neatly hung red shirt with the "stars and stripes" necktie wrapped around the hanger. "We were supposed to sneak him off. Why would he go without us?"

"There's only one answer. He's stuffed in Mom's trunk. My mother is a cold-blooded killer." The image of her mother, cold, calculating with ice water running through her veins, sent a chill down Darlene's spine. Vern was no prize, but murder?

Her thoughts were interrupted as the door handle clicked. Was Vern coming back? Where had he been? What was happening?

****

As the door opened, a maid walked in carrying a red bedspread, seemingly unaware the room was occupied. When she looked over the top of her load, her eyes widened. "Excuse, please. I think no one is here."

"You could have knocked." Robert's words were loud and harsh, but Carmen was not intimidated.

"De man who stay here ees a pig. He spill his whiskey on de bed cover. I fix." Carmen laid the accent on thick as she threw the red bedspread on the unmade bed. Smiling a vacuous smile, she looked at the two with wide, innocent eyes, hoping she was giving them the impression she was a dumb, unskilled local. The truth was, she spoke perfect English from years of teaching English as a second language. With school out for the summer, Carmen took over as head of housekeeping on the *Queen of the Seas*, a job her friend Maria held for the other nine months of the year. Maria wanted the time off and Carmen relished the chance to earn a little extra income—maybe more than she'd anticipated—with tips from rich travelers and other opportunities yet to be determined. "I clean up dis mess for you."

"That's okay." Darlene said as she snuck the whiskey filled pill bottle into her purse. "I'm not sure he's coming back."

"Why you say that?" Carmen asked.

"He's missing. No one's heard from him since last night and all his clothes are here."

"I take his clothes to a safe place. You pick them up when you leave. I come back and leave key to a locker for his clothes." Carmen walked toward the bed and started removing the rumpled sheets. "I clean de room now."

"Good idea." Robert said in his loudest voice, then turned to Darlene and whispered something Carmen couldn't quite hear.

She watched Darlene take a last look around before turning toward Carmen. "Go ahead and clean up. We'll come back for the key later. Come on, Bobby, let's go see what's happening in town."

As the door shut, Carmen Miranda began cleaning the room, leaving no trace of Gladys' earlier visit to Vern. It would take a couple of hours to remove all traces of incriminating evidence, but when she was done, this would be the last room she would ever clean. Soon she would be set for life.

****

Mary swished the ruffles of her red, white, and green Mexican skirt as she and Jack worked their way up the ramp. Jack was moving slower, but still managed to pat her backside as he followed her on the trek to their cabin. After stuffing themselves with free burritos, they'd left the family to finish their margaritas—the coupons included two per diner—Mary had only had one and Jack was sticking to water today, so no doubt Jamie, Sam, Justin, and Annie were going to be pretty giddy when they got back to the ship. One margarita had been plenty for Mary after a night of pupil patrol and sporadic sleep.

"I'm sorry to end our day so soon, dear." She fluffed the white ruffle of her new blouse. "I was ready to go out dancing in my authentic threads, but I think we both need a nap."

"I know I need to put my head down for a bit, sweetie." Jack took her hand as they strolled toward their cabin. "I hate that I'm such a party pooper."

"I gotta say this is the slowest I've seen you in the two years I've known you, but I know you'll bounce right back." Mary kept her voice strong so Jack wouldn't hear the worry behind her words. The sea air tossed her red curls as they walked. "I know you've had a long day, but let's go up to the top deck where we said, 'I do'. I want to remember that moment forever."

"I've got a few more steps in me, sweetie. It's not

that far from the elevator to our cabin, anyway." Jack took a deep breath then coughed.

"Are you sure you're okay?" Mary asked as she, too, inhaled the humid sea air.

"Smells like dead fish. Maybe this would be a good time for a cigar. Can't smell any worse." He smiled at his bride.

Mary rolled her eyes. "I can only hope the breeze will blow that stench away—the fish and the putrid cigar—but go ahead and have your damn cigar. Just wait till we get to the deck. It's just up these stairs."

Stepping up his pace, Jack rushed to the rail and pulled a cigar out of his pocket. "This is what I was going to do yesterday when I was so rudely interrupted by your ex-husband." He lit the cigar and turned to look out toward the ocean.

Mary walked up next to him and patted his sixty-nine-year-old butt. "Still got your boyish figure, dear." She leaned into him, cigar stench and all. "I love you so much."

"Yeah, me, too…" Jack's voice faded.

"That's not the enthusiastic reply I was expecting. We're only on day two of our marriage, for God's sake."

"Sorry, Mary, I just had a flash of what happened yesterday."

"With Vern? Do you remember?" Mary grabbed his shoulders, pulled him to face her, and stared into his eyes. "Tell me, Jack; tell me everything."

"I-I'm not sure I remember everything, but I do remember him punching me in the gut. I went flying across the deck and when I looked up, he was just casually leaning against this very railing. He was laughing at me like I was some insignificant piece of shit." Jack turned back to the sea and puffed on his cigar.

"That wasn't the end of it, was it? What did you do? Look at me. Tell me what you did that landed you on that hard deck with a concussion."

Eyes blazing—a look Mary had never seen—Jack answered. "I stood up, gritted my teeth, and ran toward him. He kept laughing, waving his arms, almost begging me to hit him—so I lowered my head and bashed into his disgusting beer gut. I think it hurt my head more than his gut, but his arms were flailing, and the smile left his face. He was off balance for sure and I remember wondering if he was going to fall."

"Did he fall, Jack?" Mary didn't believe Jack could have pushed a big oaf like Vern over the edge, but maybe it was a perfect hit. Maybe Vern was gone.

"I don't know." Jack's voice softened. "I don't know because I tripped and fell flat on my face."

Mary looked around. "What could you have tripped on. The deck is smooth, nothing jutting out anywhere."

"That's the funny thing. It felt more like something pulling my foot." Jack's face was red and he was dripping with sweat. "Or maybe someone."

"Oh my God. Are you sure about this?"

"I'm not sure about anything right now, sweetie." He walked over to the ashtray and stubbed out his cigar. "I'm tired—so damn tired."

"Let's not tell anyone about this. You couldn't have hurt Vern. I know it. Let's go back to our cabin so you can rest and forget all of this." Mary took his hand, leading him back to the room.

When they arrived at the cabin, Jack headed straight to bed and invited Mary to join him. As much as she wanted to cuddle her ailing husband, she knew she needed to confront her miserable excuse for an ex-husband, Vern.

"I'm not that tired, dear. I think I'll go take a walk."

Jack's eyes were closing. "Okay, sweetie. Don't be too long."

Mary watched his chest rise and fall with each breath. He was going to be okay, but she was not. She needed to find out what happened to Vern. With Jack snoring, she called the front desk and finagled Vern's room number from the ship's operator. Vern had to be there, and she was about to give him a piece of her mind.

Five minutes later, Mary knocked on the door. "Vern! Vern Bradley, you let me in." She knocked again. The third time, the door opened, but it wasn't Vern looking back. "Who are you?" Mary asked.

"I am de maid. Who are you?" The dark eyed woman had no smile for Mary.

"I'm Vern Bradley's ex-wife and I need to speak to him." Mary pushed her way into the room, a room that smelled of a lemon scented disinfectant. Vern would not be happy when he got back. He hated that smell—for forty years everything in their house had to smell of pine—forty God damn years of feeling like she was living in the middle of a forest full of pine trees.

"He ees not here, lady. Maybe he go to town."

"May I look around?" Mary asked.

"No, *señora*, you should not be here. I have to report that you push your way in."

"No, no, please. I'll leave. You probably don't understand much English, but the man who stays here is an abusive son of a bitch. I hope you're long gone when he gets a whiff of that lemon cleaner."

Mary looked around. Neat as a pin—signature Vern.

There was no way to tell whether he'd slept there last night. But why the heavy lemon disinfectant? Her cabin didn't smell that way after the maid came in. Something wasn't right.

Chapter Ten

Dead or Alive?

Darlene tugged at her tight white shorts as they left Vern's room. Robert's hand followed hers as he grabbed her exposed cheek. "Ooo, Bobby." Darlene giggled, then slapped his hand away. She loved his touch and wanted nothing more than another romp with her man, but there was no time for that now. Remembering back to their first encounter, her face flushed. She hadn't planned to feel anything real for Robert—he was just a vehicle to elevate her to financial security—but now she couldn't get enough of him.

Robert massaged his red knuckles. "You shouldn't wear those tight shorts if you want me to keep my hands to myself."

"Sorry, but we really need to get to town. The ship sails at 6:00 and it's already noon." With her shorts now covering the ass she knew was pretty damn perfect, she took Robert's hand and pulled him toward the ramp. "Are you sure we should have let the maid clean Vern's room?"

"Absolutely! If your mom killed my dad, we don't want any evidence, especially if she staged a suicide. The life insurance doesn't pay for suicide. What the hell was she thinking?"

"That's what I want to know. I've been trying to call

my mom all morning with no answer." She pulled out her phone as they walked toward the white sandy beach. "One more try."

****

Gladys sunk into the plush white lounge chair, inhaling salty sea air as she drifted toward sleep. The last twenty-four hours had taken their toll in a way she could barely fathom. Why were her hands trembling and what was that rolling wave of pain in her stomach? Nothing usually ruffled the feathers of Gladys Dunwoody, but this was different. The scheme she and Vern had devised to cash in on his life insurance had not gone as planned and now she was worried. It could still work out, but would it? She was so tired—the heavy air filled her lungs as her eyelids fell. Sleep would lay her fears to rest.

Her snoring might have woken her if her phone hadn't vibrated in her pocket first. Regretting the custom ringtone blasting *Live and Let Die*, she snorted, grabbed the phone, and answered the call. "Um, hello." Her voice was deep and groggy with sleep.

"Mom, you finally answered," Darlene said. "I've been calling all morning. What's going on?"

Gladys sat up and tried to clear her head. "Oh, I've been busy, honey. Trying to get settled. The phone must have been in the other room when you called before."

"Oh, okay. I thought you were avoiding me. Mom, I need to know if Vern ever showed up at your condo."

"No, he's not here. Maybe you and Robert should check his cabin."

"We did, Mom. It wasn't pretty."

"I'm sorry you had to find him like that. You know, he's been very depressed lately." Gladys hoped her voice conveyed the sympathy she really wasn't feeling.

"What do you mean? Vern wasn't there—just a half glass of whiskey and an empty pill bottle. Why would you think we found him? Did you think he was dead?"

Gladys was wide awake now as she flopped her legs onto the deck and stood. Pacing, she tried to find words to placate Darlene. "No, no, of course not. It's just that you said it wasn't pretty and I assumed something was wrong. Was there a note from him, telling you where he went?"

"Funny you should ask, Mom. I found a note—a suicide note."

"But no body? Vern left a note, but he wasn't there? Somebody must have moved his body," Gladys said, her voice rising with each word.

Darlene spoke slowly, emphasizing each syllable. "I found the note in *your* trunk."

"In my trunk? How did that note get in the trunk?" Gladys said without thinking. "I mean, why would a note like that be in my trunk?"

"That's what I was wondering, Mom. It looked like Vern's handwriting, but the words didn't seem like anything he would have said—I mean, can you believe he apologized for hurting the people he loved—Vern has never said he was sorry for anything. If I didn't know better, I'd think you forged the note. You were pretty good at copying his handwriting." Darlene paused. "But then I see you didn't leave it in his room, so I can't figure what you're doing."

"First of all, I would never forge a note like that," Gladys said, defending herself. "And, secondly, what the hell were you doing snooping through my trunk?"

"That's not the point, Mom. What was that note about?"

"I don't know anything about it. Vern was helping me pack. He must have put it in there," Gladys lied. "I don't know why you're so upset. Why do you care about Vern? We'd all be better off without him. If he killed himself, we wouldn't have to cover up our scheme. We'd just get the money."

"That's not true. Our insurance policy has a two year wait for suicide. It won't pay a thing, so you better hope he's still alive."

"Darlene, honey, we've had that policy on Vern for twenty years. The suicide clause doesn't apply."

"Mom, you've been gone awhile. We replaced that policy six months ago. Suicide is *not* covered, so you better tell me he's alive." Darlene's voice had an edge Gladys had never heard.

"Don't you use that tone of voice with me, Missy." Gladys snapped.

Darlene continued her slow deliberate delivery. "I'll use whatever tone I need to get to the truth. Why don't you give me your address so Robert and I can come talk to you in person. We're leaving the ship now."

"I don't see any reason for you to come over now. It's more important that we find out what happened to Vern."

"So, you're saying you have no idea where he is? Are you sure you're telling me everything, Mom?"

"I swear." Gladys said the words as she crossed her fingers. "I know nothing, honey."

"Well, okay. I guess we'll just have to wait to hear from Vern. Will you call me the minute you hear from him?" Darlene asked, her tone now sounding more settled to Gladys.

"Of course, I will. Now you and Robert go enjoy the

beach." Gladys wiped beads of sweat from her brow. "I need to go get myself a cold drink. Goodbye, dear." She hung up before Darlene could protest.

Shit! Where the hell was Vern? Gladys clung to her phone hoping it wouldn't slip though her quivering hands. No body? And how did that note get into her trunk? Maybe that was a good thing now that she knew suicide would have nullified the life insurance. She was so sure Vern was going to commit suicide—so damn sure...

****

"Bobby, now I don't know what to think." Darlene looked at her phone as if Gladys was inside. "I thought I'd get some answers from Mom, but now I have even more questions."

Robert put his arm around her shoulder. "I only heard your half of the conversation, but it sounds likes she's denying any contact with Dad. Do you believe her?"

"No, not for a second. But I do believe her plan to kill Vern somehow went awry." She turned and took Robert's face in her hands. "Your dad is still alive. I know it."

Robert bit his lip. Despite his resolve to put on a brave face, tears formed in his eyes. He pulled Darlene close and whispered, "I hope you're right."

Robert closed his eyes as Darlene wrapped her arms around his neck, laying her head against his chest. He tightened his hold, and they stood locked in their embrace while others passed them on the crowded beach. Robert didn't care if he obstructed the path or if people had to crawl over them, for that matter. Hope was alive and so, he believed, was his father.

Why Robert cared about his dad was a surprise, even to him. The guy had been an asshole through his entire childhood, taking out his frustrations on Robert, his brother Sam, and his mother, Mary. Yes, he was well aware of the damage his father had inflicted on his family both physically and emotionally and although scars from Vern's leather belt slashing his bare butt reminded him of those dark days, he still loved his dad. Maybe he deserved the discipline Vern imposed and, no doubt, he was stronger for learning life's lessons the hard way. Unlike his mother and Sam, he forgave his dad and now even thanked him for making him a better man.

Thirty years of working with Vern Bradley provided a perspective few others could appreciate. Although his father exhibited little tolerance for even the slightest mistakes Robert made as he learned the business, praise was given when due. No one else saw that side of Vern— Bradley & Son was Vern's passion, just as it had been his father's before him. When Robert finally understood the complexities of the construction industry along with Vern's personal preferences, they forged a perfect partnership. With a firm grasp on the details of the business and a loose interpretation of professional ethics, Robert became an asset to Vern. Finally, Robert gained the acceptance he'd craved throughout his childhood. No evidence of the moral fiber his mom had worked so hard to instill in her boys remained in Robert's character. A small price Robert had been willing to pay to win his father's love.

And now, he had reason to believe his dad was alive. He loosened his grip on Darlene and turned toward the ocean. The sky seemed bluer, seagulls sang as they soared overhead, the ocean's pungent aroma of salt and sea life invaded his senses. As he watched the rhythmic crashing of the waves, the tension he'd been carrying slipped from his shoulders.

"Maybe you were right. Once we get the money, we should sell what's left of the business and move down here." He leaned down to kiss her soft, full lips.

"Whatever you say, Bobby."

"Just one more obstacle. We need to get Jack arrested." Taking Darlene's hand, they continued to walk down the beach toward town.

"I know you hate Jack, but I'm feeling a little guilty pinning this on him. Couldn't we just say Vern fell overboard?"

"With no witnesses, it would take years to collect the insurance money. With Jack, I think we can convince him to confess. Once that happens, the money is ours."

"Are you sure you won't feel bad about hurting your mom?"

As much as he loved his mom, he felt a deep resentment for her now that she was sucking the business dry with her alimony checks. "I might feel bad for a moment, but I'm sure I'll get over it when the check arrives."

****

Jack woke with a start. Had it been a dream or a memory? He'd barely dozed off when the vision surfaced. He saw Vern leaning against the railing as he lowered his head and charged toward him. The impact felt as real as it had yesterday, only this time he bounced off Vern's beach ball belly in slow motion. There was time now to watch Vern raise his arms and fall backward, feet shuffling to try to right himself as he teetered back and forth. But, even in slow motion, the thing that caused him to trip last night, pulled him to the ground before he could see the result of his assault on Vern.

If this was, indeed, a memory, he'd learned one thing for sure. He and Vern had not been alone on that deck. Jack had not tripped, someone had grabbed his foot and pulled him down. That someone knew what happened to Vern.

Chapter Eleven

You Don't Know Jack

A dream or a memory? Jack wanted to believe it was a dream. It couldn't be real, he thought, as beads of sweat scattered across his forehead. But he knew in his heart—the heart that was racing with the fear—that it was, indeed, a memory. He *had* shoved Vern—more like a torpedo than a shove, really—but had it been enough to push Vern over the edge? While the charge felt like a speeding freight train to Jack, the impact may have seemed like no more than a nudge to a big guy like Vern. No, Jack didn't have the strength to cleanly dispose of Vern in one swift head butt...unless all the "what ifs" lined up. What if Vern had too much to drink and was unsteady? What if Jack had a burst of strength that even Vern couldn't withstand? What if Jack hit Vern in just the right spot throwing him off balance? What if Jack actually killed a man? Jack wiped his brow as a wave of nausea crashed through his stomach—the room's ambiguous scent of Ben Gay mixed with Mary's floral scented perfume pushed the nauseous sensation to the next level. Swallowing hard to avert the urge to vomit, he took a swig from a bottle of warm ginger ale on bedside table, Jack's remedy for indigestion.

Had he killed Vern? What was he thinking attacking a man twice his size? Jack, the man his daughters often characterized as being too passive, had never so much as touched, much less punched, another human being—until he met Mary. His love for Mary awakened a passion in him he'd never thought possible. For the past two years, he'd lived and loved with a soul penetrating fervor unmatched in his previous sixty-seven years; all because of Mary. Passion—a double edged sword—if he could love so deeply, his capacity for anger was also enhanced. And now, that passion, that anger, may have been the seed that caused him to kill another human being.

Jack thought back over his first sixty-seven years, never stepping outside or crossing any lines. Oh, he thought about it in his youth, but his father's leather strap hanging above the back door served as an effective deterrent to any wrong move. Out of fear of losing his father's respect, he never felt that black strap.

From his parents' home to his marriage to Nancy, his only inappropriate action had been pre-marital sex—the act that propelled him to the altar a little sooner than he expected. One impulsive step outside the lines colored his miserable future with Nancy. He had no regrets about the result of the pregnancy, his dear daughter, Sarah, or for that matter the second pregnancy producing daughter number two, Jamie, a few years later. Wanting to be there for his girls, he endured the first twenty years with Nancy—even as he longed for a less rigid existence. Why he stayed past the demands of parenthood, he found harder to justify. Perhaps years of criticism and guilt trips convinced him he deserved no better, or perhaps he loved Nancy despite her controlling nature. More likely, just too tired to fight it anymore, he lived a sterile existence with Nancy until the day she died. As the door closed on a cheerless chapter of his life, a new window opened when Mary popped her head full of bright red curls into Jack's view. Once he met Mary, he never looked back.

Jack's head shot off the pillow, his thoughts interrupted by the sound of the door opening ever so slowly. "Mary?"

"Yes, dear, it's me. I was trying to sneak in quietly, so I wouldn't wake you." Letting the door slam, she moved toward Jack. "Are you feeling better? You couldn't have gotten much sleep in the short time I was gone."

"I'm okay. Still got that damn headache." Jack rubbed his forehead. "Where'd you go, Mary? I hope you weren't chasing after that son-of-a-bitch ex-husband of yours."

"So, what if I was? I may be your wife, but I'm not your property, Jack Madison."

"I know that, sweetie. Boy, do I know that. I know you'll do whatever you please, but you can't stop me from worrying about you." Patting the bed, he motioned for her to sit beside him. "So, I assume you went to see Vern."

"Yes, dear, I risked my life to confront the old coot." She plopped herself next to her man and took his face in both her hands. "And I lived to tell you about it."

"So, tell me already. What did he have to say for himself?" Jack took a deep breath as his eyes widened.

"Don't get your hopes up." She dropped her hands from his face. "He wasn't there. In fact, I couldn't tell if he'd slept there last night."

"You saw his room? How'd you get in?"

"It was the weirdest thing. The maid was cleaning and it smelled to high heaven of lemon disinfectant. The sheets were off the bed and a new bedspread was folded in the corner. As I understand it, they don't change the sheets without a special request. What do you make of that?"

"I'm trying not to make anything of it. I hope she needed the disinfectant because he's a stinky pig. I need to believe he's alive and well somewhere," Jack said.

"That's what's so weird. Vern certainly has his share of shortcomings, but being a pig is not one of them. He's compulsively neat and clean," Mary said.

"Well, maybe the maid was just doing her job and overdid it with the disinfectant. Let's not worry about that old bastard." Jack swept Mary's hand to his lips, kissed each red nail, then pulled her close. "Let's consummate this marriage."

"I thought you had a headache, dear?" Mary winked as her lips curved in a wicked smile.

"I can't think of a better cure for a headache than a dose of my sweet Mary." Jack mirrored her mischievous expression as she fell into bed beside him.

****

Robert watched Darlene dress for dinner, the tight black dress arousing him once again. The margaritas at Señor Frog's had been strong—a welcome escape from the chaos Gladys and Vern had created. Things were not going as planned, but after a few margaritas, both Robert and Darlene were confident that they had this caper under control. Had Gladys killed Vern? Or was he still alive? Either way, Robert would report him missing tomorrow morning and point a finger at Jack.

Tonight, they'd have dinner with the family—the last supper, so to speak. Tomorrow, Robert would likely be excommunicated from the family and that was just fine with him. All he needed was Darlene.

"C'mon, Bobby. Time to get dressed for dinner." Looking down at his naked body, her eyes sparkled. "That is, if you can get your pants zipped.

"We could be late. Come here, honey." Robert patted the sheet beside him.

"Save it for later. I just got cleaned up." She shook her head, but Robert knew that look and he surmised she wanted him as much as he wanted her.

"Let's eat quick." What was it about Darlene? Nothing else mattered to Robert anymore. Not his brother, Sam—the perfect son who'd left home and never looked back, leaving Robert to deal with their father. Unlike Sam, he'd developed a soft spot for Vern and hoped he was still alive, but if not, he'd get over it. And he was definitely ready to separate himself from his mother—sure, she'd been a loving mom, but now her love was tainted. She betrayed Robert when she married that gold digger, Jack Madison. No, he wouldn't miss any of them as long as he had Darlene and five million dollars.

****

Mary was singing as she stepped out of the shower. The words to "Natural Woman" rolled off her tongue and seemed to hit Jack in his open heart.

He added his voice to the 'make me feel so good' line then kissed Mary's cheek as he passed her and took his place in the shower. "I think you just cured my headache, sweetie."

Twenty minutes later they were dressed and on their way to dinner. Tonight would be a challenge, as Mary had insisted on reserving a table with both of her sons. Sam was her easy child, never making waves as a kid, and as an adult, supporting her through her divorce from

Vern. Despite Sam's kind nature, putting him in the same room with Robert might prove to be a test of his patience. Hard to believe they'd been so close as kids—a bond she thought would never be broken. Now, they rarely spoke, drifting farther apart over the past ten years. Mary longed to see her boys re-kindle their bond and tonight she had high hopes of guiding them back through childhood's door—a door leading to memories that both might wish to forget. Unlike Sam, Robert had not been supportive of his mother through the divorce. Had he blocked those childhood memories? Mary hoped she could reach into his heart and resurrect his soul—it seemed he'd lost it over the past few years. Vern had done a damn good job of hardening Robert's pliable heart while extracting his soul in the less than ethical pursuit of success. Why he'd bothered to come to her wedding was a mystery, but he was here, and she was going to take this opportunity to heal the wounds of the past two years.

"There's our table, Jack." Mary pulled Jack toward the circular table, the white linen tablecloth in sharp contrast to the brightly colored cloth napkins. It was Fiesta night, but by the looks of Sam and Robert, it might as well have been night of the living dead. Without a hint of a smile, Sam was leaning away from Robert, talking to Jamie. Robert was leaning the opposite direction, whispering to Darlene.

Plucking her cell phone from her cleavage, Mary grumbled about the lack of pockets in her sequined red dress. "Okay, boys, I want a picture of you two and you better be smiling." She poised the phone to take a shot. "Come on now, look at each other and smile!"

"Aw, Mom, give it a rest." Robert said, a smirk replacing his frown.

"I mean it, Robert. That half-assed smirk won't do. Put your arm around your brother and smile. You don't have to mean it, but I want a picture of my boys as I remember you."

Sam and Robert leaned toward each other and made an awkward attempt to look joyful, tentatively touching one another's shoulders. Mary snapped a burst of photos. As the click of the camera ended, the men parted, smiles turning back to scowls.

"I hope you girls will put your men to shame and enjoy our dinner together," Jack interjected as he hugged his daughter, Jamie. "I don't believe I've met your lovely lady, Robert." He extended his hand toward Darlene.

"Darlene Dunwoody," she said as she shook Jack's hand. "I've heard so much about you, Jack."

"Darlene?" Mary asked. "Aren't you Gladys' little girl? I haven't seen your mom in years. She really kept Vern and Robert in line."

"That she did, but now that's my job," Darlene said.

Jack held Mary's chair and seated her next to Darlene, as he sat to her left, next to Jamie.

Mary laughed. "Gladys was Vern's office wife. She took care of everything, didn't she, Robert?"

Robert rolled his eyes. "You could say that. She definitely took care of Dad."

"Well, Darlene, I hope you're keeping up the good work." Mary said.

"Oh, you can bet I'm taking care of your son just like my mother took care of Vern." Darlene snickered as she reached under the table obviously hitting her target—Robert's thigh or thereabouts. Mary watched Robert squirm. It appeared Darlene was, indeed, taking care of Robert.

"Enough about the business." Sam looked at his mom and Jack. "Let's dig into these shrimp cocktails. We've been waiting for you two so we can eat!"

"Gotta say it smells great in here." Jack said.

Mary assumed he was referring to the Mexican lime chicken, cheesy refried beans, rice, and salsa, but all she could smell was Darlene's generous application of spicy-sweet perfume. It was making her gag, but she powered through the meal, all the while trying to engage her sons in civil conversation. She finally gave up and they ate most of the meal in relative silence.

As the dessert of flan and fresh strawberries was served, Mary broke the painful silence. "Robert, dear, where is your father? I went to his room to talk to him, and he wasn't there. The maid was cleaning his room like it needed disinfecting. What's going on?"

Looking directly at Jack, Robert spoke. "Why don't you ask Jack, Mom? He was the last person to see Dad."

"What are you insinuating?" Mary asked

"I'm not insinuating anything. I'm telling you without hesitation, Dad is missing, and I think Jack pushed him overboard."

"That's not possible," Sam yelled. "You know how big Dad is and Jack is barely over half his weight. How could he possibly push him over the rail?"

"Why don't you ask Jack? Dad was pretty drunk last night and very unsteady. Judging from Jack's fall, he must have been moving at a good clip. Not hard to knock over a wobbly drunk no matter how big he might be."

"Now just wait a minute." Jack jumped up from the table. "Vern punched me, and I admit I was trying to retaliate, but I tripped. I don't think I could have pushed him over."

"Maybe you better think again, Jack. I think you pushed him all right and I think I can prove it. I'll be reporting Dad missing tomorrow, so you might want to get your attorney lined up."

Chapter Twelve

No Turning Back

There would be no turning back once Robert reported his father missing. His feet felt like lead as he made his way toward the office of the Chief Security Officer, each plodding step slower than the last as he contemplated the consequences of his actions. It wasn't like he was lying—Vern was actually missing—but, alluding to the possibility that Vern had been pushed overboard might be stretching the truth. Ignoring the truth might be more accurate. Robert took a deep breath as he approached the office door. He'd find a way to say what he needed to say without lying outright; he was good at that.

Picturing his office overflowing with five million one-dollar bills cleared his head of any moral dilemma. He knocked on the door to start the ball rolling down the slippery slope.

Officer Wesley Smith opened the door to his small office, a scowl crossing his deeply tanned face when he saw Robert. "Oh, hello. I was expecting someone else." He tucked his shirt in and buttoned the top button as he gestured for Robert to come in. "What can I do for you, sir?"

"I'd like to report a missing passenger," Robert said.

"Really?" Officer Smith sighed and shook his head,

spilling a loose lock of black hair onto his forehead. "What makes you think this person is missing?"

"He got into a fight precariously close to the railing and no one has seen him since." Robert hoped the line didn't sound as rehearsed as it was.

"And you're sure not one person has seen him?" Smith asked.

"Of course, I'm sure." Robert's voice took on a deeper, more deliberate tone. "I checked with our group and no one in the family has seen him—no one." He said the words, consciously omitting his knowledge of Gladys' visit. She wasn't technically family, so it wasn't a lie.

"I understand your concern." Smith also slowed his speech, in Robert's opinion, to a condescending cadence and tone. "You know sometimes people just leave the ship in Mazatlan or Puerto Vallarta. We can't be calling foul play too soon, now can we?"

"Well, I believe we can." Robert was getting pissed. "I'm pretty damn sure he fell overboard."

"And, when did this supposedly happen?" Smith asked.

"Last night around 6:00 p.m."

"And you didn't report it then? If you were so sure he fell over, why wouldn't you report it right away?"

Robert raised his voice further, trying to keep it under control. "What good would it have done? That's a helluva drop. How would anyone survive that? Besides, no one knew what happened to him for sure—we're just putting the pieces together now. We're pretty sure another passenger pushed him overboard."

"Shit." Smith winced. "You're kidding me, right? If you're reporting a crime, I have to contact the FBI." He launched a stony stare that felt a bit intimidating to Robert. Smith continued. "Can't we just assume he got off in Puerto Vallarta and call it a day? I don't need another crime under my watch."

"Another crime? Does this happen often?"

"Not to anyone else." Smith sighed. "I'm just lucky, I guess. The wife beaters, drunks assaulting women, and petty thieves all seem to travel on my sailings. And now you want to report a homicide."

"I guess your streak of bad luck just got worse." Robert did his best to keep the smile off his face, playing the distraught son, but he felt the smile inwardly. "I absolutely want to report a homicide."

"Okay. I'll need some information." He walked toward his desk and motioned for Robert to sit. "Damn, I thought this was going to be such a nice, smooth sailing with the wedding of those nice old folks and all their family."

"Yeah, about that family. The groom is the man you'll want to talk to. He married my mother and murdered my father."

****

Robert spent the next hour completing and signing forms, while an impatient Wesley Smith looked at his watch. Either Smith did not have the authority to interrogate him, or he was rushing through the obligatory forms, so he could resume his social life. Less than ten minutes into their paperwork, a stunning young woman arrived at the cabin door, reeking of too much perfume and carrying a bottle of tequila. Wesley Smith was obviously much more interested in her than some possible dead guy. But he did his job and advised Robert that he would be hearing from the FBI.

Would he tell the FBI he'd been present and saw the whole thing? Or would he let Jack hang himself and save his eyewitness revelation if all else failed? He didn't want to perjure himself by playing the onlooker card unless he absolutely had to—his first strategy would be to encourage Jack to confess. Between Jack's concussion and his aging brain, Robert was sure he could convince Jack of his guilt. He had a few more days before the ship docked in San Francisco where the FBI would likely take Jack into custody.

Robert thought back to the incident. He was, indeed, a witness, but not to murder. As Robert watched the fight unfold, Vern played his role perfectly, setting his back to the railing, waiting for Jack's puny excuse for a head butt to "knock him over the edge." Vern was twice Jack's size—there was no way Jack had the strength to do the deed in question. But something went wrong. Robert watched as Jack launched his scrawny body toward Vern, while Vern threw his head back and laughed. Had Vern evoked superhuman strength in Jack by taunting him? Emerging from his hidden post, Robert rushed toward Jack to stop the blow, but it was too late. Jack hit the target—Vern's protruding beer gut—sending Vern teetering toward a watery grave. All Robert could do was grab Jack's ankle, stopping him from finishing the job. As Jack fell headfirst onto the deck, Robert jumped over him to grab his father's hand, pulling him to safety. Robert shoved Vern, who stumbled and swayed as they passed the staircase heading toward the elevator. With each of Vern's missteps, Robert feared discovery—he couldn't stop his dad from drinking, but he would do his best to get him out of the public eye. In his defense, Vern's bobbling along with his blank stare could have been related to his near-death experience. Whether it was the booze or the glance into his mortality, Vern promised to avoid the eyes of the wedding party and take all less travelled hallways straight to his room. That was the last time Robert saw his dad.

And now, as he made his way back to his cabin, Robert wondered if he'd ever see his father again. What was happening? Why would Vern jeopardize the plan when they'd come this far? Had Gladys actually killed him? After numerous attempts to text and call, it was clear Vern either had a dead battery or he was just plain dead.

If he was alive, there was no reason for him to hide from Robert. The only hiding Vern was supposed to do was with Gladys—in their newly purchased condo. Before the trip, both Vern and Gladys had assumed new identities and purchased the condo under assumed names, names they hadn't shared with their own children. The less Robert and Darlene knew about their parents' hideaway, the less chance of someone slipping up. But, if Gladys had really tried to kill Vern, it seemed unlikely Vern would run into her arms. Gladys wasn't answering her phone regularly either, so he might not know what the fuck was going on until they cashed in on the life insurance. Vern and/or Gladys would surely contact them when payday arrived. Robert sighed as he reached his cabin door. He needed a drink.

****

Robert wasn't surprised to see Darlene lying on the bed, sipping a martini, reading Cosmopolitan. The cover story "Everything You Need to Know About Tantric Sex" caught Robert's eye.

"I hope you're taking notes on that sex thing, honey.

I'd ask for a lesson now, but I'm exhausted." He headed toward the whiskey to pour himself a stiff one.

"You, Bobby? You're never too tired for me. What's up?" She patted the bed motioning for him to lie down next to her.

"Not me, baby." His lips curved in a half-smile. Kicking off his shoes, he followed the scent of Obsession, the fragrance that evoked all his erotic memories of Darlene. He propped himself on two pillows and slid in next to her. "I need to take a moment to process all the shit that's going on."

"No problem, Bobby." She laid the magazine down and turned her full attention to her man. "How did your meeting go?"

"I got the ball rolling. The FBI is going to come after Jack as soon as we dock in San Francisco. It's all going according to plan, so why don't I feel better?"

"The plan would be better if we knew exactly where Vern was." Darlene hesitated. "There's something I need to tell you about that."

"Something I don't know?" Robert asked as he took a healthy swig of his whiskey.

"Yeah, something really strange." She sat up and took his free hand. "Remember the maid, Carmen, was going to leave us a key to a locker, so we could retrieve your dad's clothes?"

"I remember. Did you get the key?

"I went to Vern's room and checked everywhere. There was no trace of a key or even any trace that Vern had ever been there. So, I went to housekeeping to ask about the locker. Not only was there no locker for Vern Bradley, but apparently, Carmen Miranda turned in her resignation yesterday afternoon."

"Shit." Robert closed his eyes. Darlene leaned down, kissed his forehead, and curled up next to him.

Lying there exhausted, Robert wanted nothing more than to fall asleep—to dream of a life with all the money and none of the pain he'd been running from all his life. The vibration and tri-tone ding of his cell phone brought him back to reality. He pulled the phone from his pocket.

"Darlene, are you awake?"

"Mmmmhmmm," she mumbled.

"This is big. The message is coming from Dad's phone, but it's obviously not from him."

"What does it say?"

"It says, 'I know what happened to Vern Bradley.' "

Chapter Thirteen

Revelations

Robert eyed his phone with disbelief. Finally, a message coming from his dad's phone, but it was clearly not his father. The mystery texter had just announced that he knew what happened to Vern Bradley.

—*Who is this? Where's my dad?*— Robert texted.

—*Will tell you more later. I know about your little plan. Want my share of the insurance money.*—

—*What makes you think there's money? Who is this?*—

Still avoiding identification, the texter sent another message.

—*Believe me, I know about the money. I know the whole story. Now it's imperative that Jack make a full confession. The insurance won't be paid without that*—

—*How do you know that?*— Robert punched the question into his phone.

—*I've done my research. They need a body or a confession. Nothing else will do. Text me when you've convinced Jack of his guilt and I'll tell you what happened to your dad.*—

Robert had no answer for the blackmailing texter. He set his phone on the bedside table and turned to Darlene, who had been passively reading the texts over his shoulder.

"Oh, shit, now we've got someone else involved. Who would know about the money? Who would know what happened to Dad? Who is this guy—or is it a guy?" Robert rolled off the bed and headed for the whiskey. Another shot might dull the pain of this fiasco.

Darlene stretched and pushed herself to a sitting position. Either she was still groggy with sleep, or she didn't understand the gravity of the situation. Was she really that dumb?

"Darlene? Aren't you worried about this? How can you just sit there so calmly? What the hell's wrong with you?" Boring a hole into her with his piercing blue eyes, his voice grew louder and sharper with each question.

Darlene covered her ears. "You're scaring me. I'm just as worried as you, but what can we do?"

Slamming his blue plastic *Queen of the Seas* cup on the counter produced a weak crunch, withholding the satisfaction he might have felt from the sturdy thud of a glass tumbler. Red faced with beads of sweat forming on his brow, Robert could barely control his anger. Just like my father, he thought. He had to get out of this room before he took out his rage on Darlene.

Robert spoke through clenched teeth. "I know what I'm going to do. I'm going to pay Jack a visit. I'm sure he'll come around to my way of seeing things after our conversation. He needs to prepare a full confession for the FBI and I'm going to be there to help him draft a convincing story." He inhaled deeply, keeping his gaze on Darlene. She looked like a cornered animal with her wide-eyed stare. He needed to go before he did anything to fuck things up.

"So, go already," Darlene whispered. "Please, go."

****

Despite the rise in temperature caused by the sputtering air conditioner, Darlene felt a chill. Crawling between the sheets, she pulled the scratchy red bedspread up to her chin. Robert's cologne clung to the fabric—the strong spicy scent normally set her primal urges in motion, but now a whiff of his cologne invoked a sense of panic. Inhaling the offensive odor conjured images of his tight lips and laser focused blue eyes, a look she would not soon forget. Was Robert turning into his father? Were anger and abuse carried in the genes? Was it just a matter of time before Robert laid his hands on her in a less than loving way? She had never feared Robert in all the years she'd known him—until today.

And now, as they neared the resolution of their scheme, she would be tied to Robert for life. Not that she wanted to leave—she truly loved her Bobby—but she couldn't help wondering what kind of life it would be if things didn't go his way. All the money in the world wouldn't be worth black eyes and broken bones—and there would be no escape. She knew too much.

She pulled the covers over her head and curled into a fetal position. She needed her mom—or better yet, she needed a good nurturing mom to comfort her—that was certainly not her mother. Feeling wet streaks running down her cheeks, Darlene touched her face. What the hell was happening to her—tears hadn't leaked from her violet-blue eyes since her eighteenth birthday—the last time she let her mother push her buttons. She'd developed a thick skin over the years, but now she broke down and sobbed.

****

The knock on the cabin door caused Jack to trip over his half pulled up swim trunks; Mary steadied him as he pushed his leg through. Their morning had been spent re-consummating their marriage and Jack had to say he was feeling much better. The headache had all but disappeared and although his recollection of the other night was still sketchy, he had a feeling he'd done no harm. Life was good!

"Who the hell's knocking on our door?" Jack groused. "The kids are meeting us at the pool, aren't they?"

"Yes, dear, that was my understanding." Mary shot a loving look at her man as she walked toward the door. "It's probably the maid coming to change our sheets." She winked at Jack.

Jack smiled at his new bride, then immediately tensed as she opened the door to reveal her son, Robert. What was he doing here?

"Hello, Mother." Robert said in what seemed to Jack a rather formal tone. "Hello, Jack."

"We were just heading to the pool." Mary's voice seemed overly cheerful as she motioned him into the room. "Why don't you join us?"

"I'm not much of a swimmer. You know that, Mother." Robert switched his gaze from Mary to Jack. "It's you I want to talk to, Jack."

"Me, why me?" Jack had a hard time controlling his anxiety around Robert—there was something about him that always made him uncomfortable. Jack steadied his voice. "I don't think we have anything more to talk about. Didn't you say everything last night at dinner?"

"Not quite everything." Robert's voice was deep and strong. "I think you need to reconsider your position. I've talked to security, and it seems several passengers reported seeing something—or someone—fall

106

overboard right around the time you and my dad were fighting."

"That can't be." Jack had just convinced himself he didn't have the strength to push Vern overboard. "I couldn't possibly have pushed your big fat father over the edge."

"And, why not? You, yourself said you didn't see the outcome of your actions," Robert said.

"No, no I couldn't have. Oh my God, did I?" Jack sat on the bed, leaned forward, and held his head in his hands. His voice almost inaudible, "No, I'm not a killer. I am not."

Mary rushed to his side and sat so close to him he could feel the buttons on her swimsuit. "Dear, you didn't do anything. I know you. You wouldn't hurt a fly." She wrapped her arm around him as he shuddered.

"Mother, you're going to have to accept the fact that Jack killed the father of your children."

"No, I won't accept it!" Mary screamed. "I won't."

Jack sat up and patted Mary's leg. "He may be right, sweetie. I may have killed Vern."

"Of course, I'm right, Jack. All the evidence points to you." Robert laughed, which seemed eerily out of place. "Maybe you'll get off easy, Jack—manslaughter or maybe even self-defense, if you're lucky. The judge may take pity on an old man—I hope not, but even I've got to admit that's a possibility." Robert's twisted smile gave Jack the creeps. What was wrong with this guy, surely Mary hadn't borne this kid. Robert wasn't about to let up. "I'd like to see them lock you up for life, but I'll settle for a couple of years—enough to get you the hell out of our lives."

"Robert!" Mary yelled. "You will not talk to my

husband that way."

"I'll talk to that murderer any way I want. Hopefully, you'll divorce the bastard once they put him away."

"I'll never do that. Vern deserved whatever he got," Mary said. "Jack was only defending himself."

Robert's eyes widened, eyebrow arching. "So, you think he did it, huh?"

"I didn't say that, at least I didn't mean that. Oh, God, what's happening here?"

"It's okay, sweetie." Jack felt suddenly calm. "I think Robert may be right. I think I did push him over."

"You bet you did." Robert said. "And, by the way, the FBI will be waiting for you when we dock in San Francisco."

"I'll be ready." Jack stood, his eyes boring into Robert's steely blue gaze. "Now you get the hell out of here."

Chapter Fourteen

Payback

Gladys ran her fingers over one of Darlene's grade school paintings as she continued to empty her trunk. The image of "mommy and me," as Darlene had named it, brought a smile to Gladys' lips, tinged with a pang of guilt. Years of parental missteps tugged at her heart, but that was nothing compared to the anxiety she felt over her attempt to kill Vern. At the time it seemed reasonable—payback for all the years she endured sleeping with the big oaf—the price she'd paid to provide a better life for her and her daughter. And now, the scent of salt air drifting through her new condo reminded her it had been worth letting Vern climb into her bed three times a week for thirty-five years, but not worth one more day. Yes, Vern provided a more than generous salary in exchange for her services both in and out of the office and when added to the money she embezzled over the years, she would be quite comfortable. But she wanted more than basic comfort— Vern's death promised enough money to live in luxury. Closing her eyes, she imagined two million dollar bills floating and swirling through her bedroom onto her soft, king sized bed. The feelings of arousal she felt when she thought of the money quelled any anxiety she'd been feeling over Vern's untimely demise.

She, Darlene, and Robert would share the wealth now that Vern was really dead—or was he? Confused by the fact that no one had reported finding his body, Gladys wondered if Robert was scheming to cut her out of the plan. Or worse, had Vern survived the Ambien laced whiskey she served him two nights ago? No, that wasn't possible. She'd done the math—no one could rise from that many Ambien tablets in a shot of Jack Daniels. Someone must have found his body, but who and why wouldn't they report his death?

As Gladys plodded through the contents of the trunk, she found a valentine from Vern. Why hadn't she thrown that thing out? Probably because she had once loved the big lug and this valentine was proof that he had a good heart under his gruff coat of armor. Not one for sentimental syrup, Gladys had laughed at Vern that day and now as she remembered the image of his downturned eyes and sunken shoulders, she almost shed a tear. He'd never given her another card, but Gladys knew he loved her. Perhaps she'd been a bit hasty in sending him to his grave.

****

After Robert left their room, Jack searched Mary's eyes, squirming under their scrutiny. He saw something he'd never seen before as her soft green eyes transformed into flashing emeralds under her furrowed brow. What were her eyes trying to reveal? Anger? Disapproval? Disappointment?

"What is it, Mary?" He wanted to turn away, but his eyes held her searing gaze.

"You're not really going to confess to Vern's murder, are you?" Mary's sharp, staccato words grated on Jack's ears. She was clearly not happy with him.

"Of course not, sweetie." Jack smiled hoping to temper the sting of Mary's angry eyes. "I don't know if I pushed Vern over the edge, but I don't think I did."

"Then why did you say you were going to confess?"

"Because your son, Robert, wouldn't have settled for anything short of an admission of guilt."

Mary finally blinked. "Oh, thank God. You were damn convincing, Jack Madison. Even I believed you were ready to confess."

"Not on your life! We're gonna fight this all the way." Jack squeezed her hand and leaned in for a kiss.

Mary touched his face with her free hand and kissed him softly. "Let's go meet the rest of the kids—the ones who actually like us—at the pool."

"I'm ready. Race you to the swim up bar. I could really use a margarita." Jack licked his lips, imagining the salty rim of that sweet margarita.

"You must be feeling better, dear. Catch me if you can." Mary laughed, grabbed her beach bag, and ran for the door.

****

The vibration of Gladys' phone in her pocket brought her back to the present. Who the hell wanted to talk to her now? Was Darlene going to keep bugging her? She pulled the phone into view and there it was—a text message from Vern! Oh my God, he was alive. This was going to be a difficult conversation...

Vern: —*Are you surprised to hear from me, Gladys?*—

Gladys: —*Of course not. I was just wondering where you were. What happened?*—

Vern: —*Don't you remember? You tried to kill me.*—

Gladys: —*How so? I just put your Ambien in your whiskey like I always do. Didn't you sleep well?*—

Vern: —*One Ambien might have been okay, but the bottle was empty, honey. I could have died.*—

Gladys: —*Someone must have come in after me. You know I wouldn't do that to you.*—

Vern: —*Someone did come in after you and saved me. I was so grateful I told her about our plot. Now she wants a big cut of the insurance money – $200,000.*—

Gladys: —*That's only 10%. We can do that.*—

Vern: —*Really?*—

Gladys: —*What do you mean 'Really'? You know the cut. 2 mil for us and 3 mil for Robert and the business.*—

Vern: —*Yeah, sorry, honey. Of course.*—

Gladys: —*Who is this captor? Is this really you, Vern?*—

Vern: —*Of course, it's me, honey. I need to go now. I'm gonna get caught. I'll text you later.*—

Gladys looked at the phone. Vern was alive—or was he? Looking at the bubbles of text, she knew those words had not come from him. He had never, ever called her honey. It was always Darlin' or Glad—in thirty-five years there had never been a "Honey"—until today. His captor was texting from his phone, but who was this person? And was Vern dead or alive?

Chapter Fifteen

Right Place Right Time

Two days earlier:

When Ramone Garcia turned up drunk to work again, Carmen was more than annoyed. Granted, this was his second job—as a busboy through two dinner shifts, he often made a habit of emptying half-full glasses of beer and wine into his gullet rather than down the sink. On this night, too many sippers left their spoils for Ramone, leaving him barely able to walk. His job with Carmen called for him to place *Queen of the Seas* mints on the passengers' pillows and turn down the sheets, a simple job, but not so simple if you can't tell a chocolate mint from a rabbit turd. As head of housekeeping, Carmen either had to find a replacement or do it herself.

As fate would have it, the job was left to Carmen to deliver the foil wrapped chocolate mints to Ramone's block of fifty rooms. Most travelers were off to the casino or dancing the night away, so the task moved along smoothly—a knock on the door, no answer, then Carmen used her master key, whisked into the room, turned back the red bedspread, and placed a mint on each pillow. Rarely, someone would answer their door, whereas she would hand the passenger the mints and offer to turn back the coverlet. After forty-two rooms, she knocked on Vern Bradley's door—no answer—she swiped her key, opened the door and there he was laid out on the bed wearing nothing but his red, white, and blue briefs.

Was he sleeping? Her first instinct was to back out quietly, but something told her there was more to this guy's story. Hoping he wouldn't wake up, she inched closer, the beat of her heart pulsing in her ears. The large gut on this man should have been rising and falling with his breathing, but the fleshy mound showed no discernable movement.

Should she touch him or call for help? In the interest of time, she opted to proceed on her own—her CPR training would serve this poor man's needs more efficiently than calling the ship's doctor. Carmen took his wrist firmly in her hand eliciting a muffled groan from the man's lips and a weak, tinny pulse beneath her touch. He was alive.

An envelope rested on the bedside table next to a half empty glass of what smelled like whiskey. An empty pill bottle stood neatly by, forming the final clue to an apparent suicide. Not today, Carmen thought. This guy is not going to die on my watch.

"Sorry, *señor*." Carmen slapped his face, hoping to rouse him, but not to rile him. "Time to wake up, Mister." She slapped him again and jumped back.

Vern stirred, but clearly, he was not going to lash out at Carmen. She knew what she had to do. Running to the bathroom, she grabbed a hand towel, soaked it in cold water, and hurried back to place it on the man's forehead—evoking a moan as he rolled his head. Next, she filled a blue plastic tumbler with water, knowing it would take more than one drink to flush the poison from this man's body. His head felt like a lead weight as she tried to tip him toward the water, pouring it down his throat as he sputtered and dribbled the liquid down his chin. Using all the pillows on the bed, she propped him upright while she raced to refill the tumbler with another cleansing load. She did that four more times, then headed for the coffee maker to brew a strong pot of coffee. The pungent aroma of the double strength Mexican blend filled the room as she checked the passenger list to secure the identity of this man.

"Mr. Bradley? Are you Vernon Bradley?" A slow nod from Vern confirmed he was indeed the passenger assigned to this room. After three cups of the strong caffeine remedy, Vern Bradley appeared to be heading toward revival. But Carmen Miranda's work was not done.

"Stand up, *señor*." Carmen used both hands to grab his large, sausage-like fingers. "Come with me."

Vern stared at her as if he didn't quite understand the words, but did as he was told, his legs at first buckling under him as he tried to stand. With Carmen's guidance, he managed to stagger to the bathroom where she pushed him into the shower stall and turned on the cold water.

"What the fuck?" Vern growled as he jumped free of the downpour and shook his mop of greasy hair. His eyes popped open as he steadied his glare on Carmen. "Damn, woman, who the hell are you and what are you doing?" Her eyes met his then dropped to his wet briefs—he immediately placed his hands over his crotch.

Carmen lifted her gaze back to his eyes. "I am your savior, *señor*." She reached for his hand, and apparently giving up his modesty, he let her guide him back to the bed. Even in his flaccid state, Carmen could see he had a package most women would find surprising and despite his obtrusive gut, she found this man attractive. "You need more coffee, but I think you will survive." He was a big man, and the whiskey was only half gone—obviously he'd passed out before he ingested a lethal dose of the drugs.

While Vern poured more coffee down his throat, Carmen picked up the envelope on the bedside table and sat next to him. She read the note, complete with apologies to his family—it was clear he wanted to commit suicide. But if that were true, why didn't he just drink the whiskey in one shot and be done with it?

"Mr. Vern? You were trying to kill yourself?" she asked as she touched his free hand.

"Oh, God, no! Why would you think that?" Vern reached for the note. "Let me see that." Reading "his" words, he bristled. "I didn't write this note."

"Then who did?"

"The only woman who can mimic my handwriting, Gladys Dunwoody." His eyes grew wide as the blood rushed to his face. "That bitch tried to kill me."

"Should we report this to the captain?" Carmen asked.

"Oh, no, we should handle this ourselves." Vern was obviously regaining his strength as evidenced by his deep resonant tone—a tone that had Carmen questioning her safety.

"What do you mean? You're not going to kill this Gladys, are you?" Carmen had done her good deed for the day, now she needed to get out before she got in too deep. She didn't want to know any more. Her voice quivered as she took a step toward the door. "I should go. I let you take care of Gladys without me. I say nothing, okay?"

"Wait." Vern grabbed her wrist, a bit too tightly, she thought. Her heart was racing. What had she gotten herself into?

She tried to pull away. "No, I go, *señor*. Please, let me go. I saw nothing."

Vern loosened his grip as he looked into her wide, frightened eyes. "Take me with you. I need to get out of here unnoticed."

"I can't take you home with me. I do not know you and I do not want to be involved in this." She pulled her hand free but didn't run. For some reason she trusted Vern—just not enough to help him out. "You will be okay, *señor*."

"But I need your help. I have nowhere to go. I was supposed to go to Gladys' condo. I'm not ready to face her, but I do need to let her know her plan failed. Do you have a master key?"

"Yes. Why?" Carmen asked

"I need you to take this letter to her room. If she's not there, open her trunk and put it right on the top. That way she'll know her plot to kill me failed." Vern laughed. "Won't she be surprised when she finds that note."

"Oh, no, I couldn't do that. I need to go." Carmen stood up and walked toward the door.

Vern's voiced followed her as he asked, "Would $50,000 change your mind?"

"What?" Carmen's head spun around, her eyes landing on Vern's stone-cold expression. A chill fluttered through her spine as she focused on his intense gaze, then a thrill when the dollar amount registered in her brain. "$50,000? Are you a rich man?"

"Not yet, but I will be soon."

"How soon? Why should I help you if you don't even have the money? Tell me how you plan to pay me." The rush she felt a moment earlier was fading at the thought of waiting for her payday. She reached for the doorknob.

"Wait. Just listen a minute. When I go missing, assuming you can get me out of here without detection, a man will likely be accused of my murder. When that happens—and it will—my son will collect my life insurance. I'll share that with you if you help me."

Carmen's eyes travelled from his head to his huge feet. "You are a big man. It will not be easy to sneak you out. Exactly how much life insurance do you have?"

"Five mmm…er…hundred thousand dollars, but most of that has to go to pay off my business debts."

"That is a lot of money. If I help you and keep this quiet, I need half." Carmen knew she was in the driver's seat now. She could ruin his plans if she turned him in, but there was no need to tamper with his scheme if it meant she could clear $250,000.

"I'll give you $200,000 if you get me out of here and hide me for a while. Is that enough to keep you quiet, darlin'?"

"I will let you know in the morning. I will be back at 7:00 a.m. to give you my answer." Turning the knob on the cabin door, she let herself out.

****

Vern hadn't slept well after the woman left, still groggy from the drugs, but highly caffeinated. His eyelids would start to droop, then pop open as the caffeine-induced anxiety set his mind reeling. Not only had he failed to get the woman's name, he had no idea how he was going to escape without someone recognizing him. At his size, an observant passenger was bound to remember him if he were to walk off in his street clothes. How the hell was he going to fake his death if he couldn't get off the ship without being seen? Would this woman be back to help him? It was 6:45 a.m. In fifteen minutes, he would know if he had an accomplice. He pulled the red bedspread up to his chin and closed his eyes, hoping for a few minutes of rest. The stench of his own sweat mixed with the smell of stale whiskey and coffee grounds finally pushed Vern over the edge. He needed a shower—a hot soapy one this time.

Vern staggered to the shower, thanking his big fat gut for providing enough volume to soak up the overdose of Ambien. Despite feeling a little weak, he knew he'd live to see the day Gladys would pay for her little stunt—if one could call a murder attempt a stunt. As the hot water saturated his clammy skin, he closed his eyes letting the stream of hot liquid plaster his thick black hair to his cheeks. Despite his anger, or maybe because of it, it felt good to be alive—even if he had to play dead for a while.

Stepping out of the shower, he was greeted by the woman who had saved his life.

"Good morning, Mr. Vern, I see you're feeling better." Her eyes took in his full naked body as she extended her hand. "Let me introduce myself. I am Carmen Miranda and I have decided to help you."

Vern didn't know whether to cover his package or reach out to shake her hand. "What the hell. You've seen it all." He shook Carmen's hand.

"Come with me. I will dress you for your escape."

****

Thirty minutes later, Vern and Carmen were ready

119

to go. Carmen peeked out the doorway and saw the hallway was empty. She held the door open as Vern rolled the guides on the wheelchair Carmen had secured, propelling himself into the hallway. No one would recognize him with the big, floppy hat and sunglasses— and that red bedspread with the ruffle at the bottom looked like the kind of big, full skirt an old woman would wear. The scarf around his face and the Mexican shawl across his chest finished the look. Carmen shut the door and proceeded to wheel Vern toward the ramp that would lead to his disappearance.

Chapter Sixteen

Last Day at Sea

"I love you, Mary Madison." Jack tightened his grip on Mary's waist as they set their eyes toward the sea, the briny path leading them back to San Francisco's harbor.

Mary turned her face to her new husband. Jack sensed her eyes on him, but knew he'd break if he looked her way. "Jack, please look at me."

"I can't. If I turn your way, it will feel like our wedding and God knows, I don't feel like the same man you married." He continued to face forward, breathing in a chest full of salty sea air. "I'm so sorry, sweetie."

"For what? For defending yourself against my disgusting ex-husband. I'm the one who should be sorry. If you hadn't met me, this would never have happened."

Jack finally turned his tear-stained face toward the woman who had changed his life in every way. "If I hadn't met you, I'd never have known the depth of true love. Whatever happens, I will not regret my life with you. You stole my heart."

"And I'm not giving it back. We will get through this." She touched his damp cheek. "You sound like a man who's expecting the worst."

"Maybe I am…" Jack turned back to the ocean, watching the powerful waves slow the path to his destiny. The reflection of the morning sunlight hit Jack between his eyes, awakening every anxious thought floating through his concussed head. Would he spend his last twenty years with his sweet Mary, holding her every night till "death do us part" or would he wither away in prison never again to know her soft touch?

Jack pulled Mary close as they leaned against the railing—a railing too tall for height challenged souls like the two them to fall over easily, but likely too short to hold Mary's much taller ex-husband. God, Jack hated that asshole for putting Mary through all those years of abuse. And now that she was finally safe from Vern's heavy hand, Jack might be deserting her for a jail cell. Did he kill Vern? He would probably never know for sure, but he did know that, even in death, Vern continued to control Mary's destiny.

"Do you think I have the strength to push Vern over this railing?" Flexing his arm to show off his bicep, he smiled.

"I love you, dear, but I really don't think you're a match for Vern." She squeezed his flexed bicep. "Strong for an old man—wiry but tough. Not sure if all that strength could shove a big, burly tub of goo like Vern over the edge, though."

"I hope you're right, sweetie." Jack was rarely at a loss for words, but he couldn't get out of his head. He kept seeing Vern teetering on the railing, looking even taller than his six-foot-two-inch height, waving his arms and smirking—a cartoon-like figure mocking him. Then the pull on his ankle dropped his face on the deck, robbing him of the final view. What the hell happened?

Interrupting his spiraling thoughts, Mary's voice, competing with the increasing headwinds, was barely audible to Jack's failing ears. "Let's savor our last few hours at sea."

Jack gently tipped Mary's face in his direction, silently noting the tears pooling in her emerald-green eyes. "I only want to think of you right now. Only you." Jack said as Mary laid her head on his chest and wrapped her arms around him with a grip so tight his breath caught. Sliding his fingers through her silky red curls, he wondered if this would be the last day he would hold this woman in his arms.

****

Five days had passed since Carmen rescued Vern. Saving his life was the easy part—his ample size allowed him to tolerate a large amount of Ambien without consequences. She'd merely awakened him from a deep sleep and in the process gained access to a secret that could net her $200,000.

"More sangria, Mr. Vern?" Carmen raised the pitcher as they sat at her small kitchen table, the aroma of her homemade burritos and refried beans filling the air.

"I'd rather have a beer, but if that's all you've got, fill 'er up." He cocked his head and smiled. "By the way, what's the occasion? Why did you decide to let me out of my room?"

Pouring the sangria into Vern's glass, she returned his smile. "I don't mean to keep you a prisoner, *señor*, but until your family agrees to pay me, I need to keep you here."

"Then give me back my phone and I'll talk to them. Why won't you let me handle this, darlin'?" He winked and reached for her hand.

Carmen slapped away his advance. "I am disturbed by some things your son and this Gladys woman are

123

saying. They think they are talking to you when I text them and I get a feeling there is much more money than you are telling me."

"Isn't $200,000 enough for you? Before you met me, you had nothing." His smile faded.

Carmen felt a chill as she studied his eyes but moved forward with her interrogation. "I am taking a big risk by harboring you. I will have to pay my friend in internet security for his manipulation of ship records—probably with my flesh—just so you will not show in the computer system as leaving the ship. As far as the records go, you never left and since you are missing, the only logical answer is that you fell—or were pushed—overboard. I am your savior, Mr. Vern, and without me, you would have nothing."

"If I got rid of you, no one would be the wiser." Vern's face turned red as his hands formed fists.

Carmen remained calm despite the fear rising within her. "You will not do that. You are a schemer, not a killer. Besides, you would have to kill my son, too. He had a lot of questions when he picked you up from the ship in your red bedspread and floppy hat."

"Where is Javier anyway? Without him here to protect you, I could just leave."

"And where would you go, *señor*? To Gladys, the woman who tried to kill you?" Their eyes locked. "Or maybe I should just turn you in to the police."

"I haven't done anything wrong—yet. The police have nothing on me…but maybe I could stay here a few more days." Vern lifted his glass of sangria, took a big gulp of the fruity wine, and dug into his plate full of burritos. "You're a damn good cook, woman. I might even stay here longer if you'd give me a little more freedom."

"And why should I trust you? What did you have in mind?"

"Just lose the lock on the bedroom door. Where am I going to go? And maybe let me use my phone once in a while."

"I'll think about it." For some reason, Carmen didn't think Vern would run off, but she wasn't ready to give him full freedom, yet.

Carmen might leave the door unlocked when her son was home. He wasn't as big as Vern but was much stronger. Javier would make sure Vern didn't go anywhere, that is unless he was drunk or stoned—which he often was. No, she could not afford to leave the door unlocked at this point and she damn well was not going to give Vern his phone. She still had a few questions for both Robert and Gladys. Yes, $200,000 was a lot of money, but maybe she'd get a raise—her gut told her there was a lot more money for the taking.

****

Robert spent the last few days of the cruise trying to convince Darlene he was not a monster like his father. When he raised his voice—and almost raised his hand to her—he watched her recoil like an infant seeking her mother's womb. He loved Darlene and despite his lack of morals and ethics in every other aspect of his life, he felt a fierce and pure loyalty to this woman. As she held his heart hostage, he begged her forgiveness not only with words, but with pricey baubles from the ship's Duty-Free store. Now, she was finally back in his bed, her gaze firmly focused on the diamond encrusted bracelet wrapped around her wrist.

"Do you really love me, Bobby?" Her eyes moved

from the shiny jewels to Robert propped on his pillow next to her. His ice-blue eyes held hers.

"You know I do, baby." He touched her cheek with a softness even he didn't know he was capable of. He was used to their passionate, almost rough, exchanges, but he wanted to prove to her that he would never hurt her.

She touched his hand and snuggled closer. "I believe you. I love you, too. Don't ever scare me like you did."

"I didn't mean to, baby. I was just so frustrated with all this shit." As he thought of the convoluted events of the week, a surge of the anger came bubbling to the surface. He wanted to lash out; instead, he did his best to diffuse the feeling with a deep breath. "I'll never hurt you—never. You are the one good thing in my life."

"Everything's going to be all right, Bobby. In a few months we'll have all we need."

Chapter Seventeen

Halfway Home

Jack handed his cruise card to the security agent as he and Mary prepared to leave the ship for the last time. The system was simple, when the bar code was swiped, the computer brought up a picture of the traveler, the security agent compared the likeness to the person standing in front of him and that was the end of it. Not this time. The agent's eyes widened as he looked at the screen and then at Jack, prompting him to wave toward a man in a dark suit standing just ahead.

"You need to stay right here. I was told I was going to have a murder suspect pass through, but you're the last person I would have suspected." His hand shook as he returned Jack's card.

"Would it help if I told you the guy deserved it?" Jack chided himself for his unfortunate choice of words. "Not that I did anything. I'm not a murderer." He corrected in a voice a little too loud.

"Keep your voice down." Mary said in a hushed tone as she watched other passengers turn when they heard the exchange.

"May I have your card, ma'am. If you're his wife, I believe you'll need to stay behind for an FBI escort as well."

Mary complied and within seconds, the man in the

dark suit rushed to them, snapping handcuffs on Jack as he led them both off the ship. Special Agent Matt Hansen had no smiles for either of them. He stopped only to let Mary point out their luggage which another agent pulled aside, opened, and painstakingly examined each item in their multiple suitcases. After determining there were no weapons hidden in Mary's lingerie or wrapped in Jack's Hawaiian shirts, the contents were stuffed back into the bags and loaded into the van that would take them downtown.

Arriving at FBI headquarters in San Francisco, Jack and Mary found they were not alone. The entire wedding party had been stopped as they left the ship and now, they were all here, seated on hard wooden chairs in the stark waiting area. Everyone, except Robert and Darlene.

Jack felt the strain of the handcuffs, binding his hands uncomfortably behind his back. Between the restraints and his fall earlier in the week, his arthritic joints were screaming in pain.

"Any chance you could release me from these God damn handcuffs, Detective Hansen? I promise I won't run. And, even if I tried, do you really think I could outrun you guys and your guns?" Jack pleaded his case in a tone he hoped Mary wouldn't see through. But despite his effort to show a brave face, she didn't seem to be buying his bravado.

"Please let my husband have his dignity. He's not a threat, for God's sake." Mary's eyes captured Jack's gaze, looking so deeply into his soul he had to turn away. Did he see pity in those green eyes? That was the last thing he wanted from Mary. He wasn't going to cry, damn it.

In only a few days, her ex-husband had changed

everything. Whether he was still alive or lying at the bottom of the ocean, he'd managed to continue his long-standing torture of Mary and now Jack was on the receiving end as well.

Detective Hansen was a big, burly guy whose lips hadn't curved upward into any semblance of a smile since they'd met, but apparently, he had a heart or maybe it was just common sense. He looked from Jack to Mary and back to Jack. "I don't see you as a flight risk, especially with that guy at the door with his finger on his gun. I think we can remove the handcuffs for now." He seemed to be trying not to smile as he removed the restraints. Funny, no one saw Jack as a physical threat, and yet he was being questioned for possibly pushing the biggest guy on the ship overboard.

Once the restraints were removed, Jack found his arms free to hug his daughters who had risen from the butt-numbing wooden seats and were surrounding him. Sam, David, and Aunt Dot completed the circle, forming a protective wall around Jack and Mary.

"Group hug," Aunt Dot announced. Leave it to her to make this a happy reunion, Jack thought as he complied with Dot's command.

A tension relieving sigh from Mary and hesitant laughter from the rest gave Jack a moment of relief from the fear of his unknown future.

"Go ahead and laugh, everyone. Let it out." Jack laughed almost too loudly, but he'd held his feelings in so long, he could barely control his giggles. That started a chain reaction as Jamie snorted, Sam's deep laugh resonated, and Jack and Mary both had tears running down their cheeks from laughing so hard. Aunt Dot's signature cackle kept the swell of laughter flowing.

"What the hell is so damn funny?" Robert roared as he emerged from the interrogation room. "You won't be laughing when this is over, Jack." Darlene clung to Robert's side, her eyes wide with fear—or was it guilt—Jack couldn't get a read on her. Robert, on the other hand, wore a grin that looked more like a victory smirk than a welcoming smile. What had happened in that interrogation room, Jack wondered?

Mary spoke. "We were just trying to ease the tension. You're my son, Robert, and I love you, but why are you trying to make this so difficult for Jack? You know he wouldn't kill a fly."

"I don't know that at all, Mom. In fact, I believe he killed my father. You have no idea what kind of man you married."

Mary scowled as she faced Robert. "Oh, yes, I do. You're wrong about him. But maybe I've been wrong about you. You're not the sweet little boy I gave birth to forty-five years ago. What happened to you?"

Robert's smirk faded. "I'd love to stay and debate this issue with you, Mom, but we have a plane to catch." He turned to Jack. "Good luck, Jack. You'll need it."

****

Robert pulled on Darlene's hand to get her out the door before she could say anything—or give them that pathetic, guilty look. "Come on, Darlene. Don't look back. Let's just get out of here."

"You don't need to pull so hard. I'm coming." Darlene stumbled in her high heels. "I feel kind of bad for your mom."

"She'll be fine, especially after Jack is convicted. She'll get a cut of the insurance money to pay off her alimony in one big fucking lump sum." Robert dropped

Darlene's hand as they got to the elevator and slammed his fist against the button. "God, after all these extra payments, will there be any money left to save the business?"

"Five million is a lot of money, Bobby." Darlene bit her lip, seeming to hesitate before she went on. "It looks like it will be all but assured with your eye-witness testimony. I know you want that money, but aren't you worried about getting caught in a lie?"

"I'm not going to wait for Jack to confess. I thought I had him convinced he did it and should give himself up, but now I'm not so sure. He seems to be having doubts about his guilt."

"Probably because deep down he knows he didn't do it. I can't say as I blame him for not confessing." Darlene jumped as the elevator door opened to a loud ding.

"You're going to blow everything if you don't calm down." Robert grabbed her arm and pulled her into the empty elevator.

"How can I calm down when I witnessed you lie to the FBI? You should have let Jack hang himself. He was so unsure of himself they would have assumed he was covering something up. You probably perjured yourself for no reason and now how can I testify without lying? Damn it, Robert, you're making this harder than it should be." Darlene pulled away from his tightening grip.

Robert's face turned red as his eyes narrowed. "You're getting a little too lippy, woman. I'm still your boss."

"Give me a break. We're so far past that. Your mom may have been a doormat to your dad, but I'm not going to let you do that to me."

"My mom is the reason I had to lie. There's no way in hell she would have let Jack confess. She's definitely not a doormat anymore." Robert wrung his hands. He'd inherited his penchant for anger from his dad and it was boiling close to the surface. He had to control it. Darlene wouldn't take another outburst and he knew it. He held his tongue as they exited the elevator but held her hand a little tighter than he should have. She winced and turned her eyes downward remaining silent. He was back in control of both his anger and Darlene.

"Looks like our Uber is here. We're looking for a blue Honda CR-V," Robert announced as he nudged Darlene toward the exit door. "Go tell the driver I'll be there in a minute. Gotta grab our luggage from security."

Darlene nodded but didn't speak. It was going to be a long ride to the airport.

Chapter Eighteen

Stuck in San Francisco

Special Agent Hansen fixed his gaze on Jack as he escorted Sarah and David to the waiting room. Hansen's raised eyebrow and stoic nod were clear signs he and Mary were next, but the man would just have to wait while Jack said goodbye to his daughter and son-in-law.

"Bye, Dad." Sarah lunged toward her dad, wrapping him in a hug that threatened to suck the last breath from his lungs. Did she know something he didn't know? She pulled back momentarily, her damp eyes telling Jack she had a story he wasn't sure he wanted to hear. "We're going to head to the airport. Text us when you're on your way."

"Let's hope the interrogation doesn't take too long," Jack said in the cheeriest voice he could muster.

"The flight is still three hours away." David said. "Talk fast so we can get you home."

Jack threw a sideways glance at Agent Hansen whose face was unreadable—no smile, no hint of what was to come. Jack turned back to his daughter. "Don't let them close the doors without us. We'll be there." It was a promise he wasn't sure he'd be able to keep.

Hansen nodded. "We're ready for you, Jack. Mary, you'll have to wait outside."

Mary's voice rose a few decibels. "Not so fast,

Hansen. I will be acting as Jack's counsel. Will that get me in the room?"

"You're not an attorney, are you?" Hansen asked.

"I don't believe that's a requirement. I've been on the internet checking and a person can hire anyone they choose to represent them. Jack chooses me," Mary said with an authoritative tone Jack admired. He loved this woman before, but the degree of his love and respect rose to new heights with her fervent plea.

"Is that right, Jack? You want your wife to hear all this?"

"You bet your ass I want this woman to represent me." Reaching for Mary's hand, Jack laced his fingers through hers and pulled her close. Her free hand seemed to swing in slow motion to cradle Jack's face as he whispered, "We got this, sweetie. We got this."

Jack said the words, wishing he could believe they were true as he and Mary followed Agent Hansen to the interrogation room. God it was depressing. No pictures, no plants, nothing but a well-worn wooden table and a few wobbly chairs. The stench of pine scented aerosol, obviously used to cover up the body odor of previous interviewees, filled the small room. Jack coughed while Mary covered her nose with her hand.

Looking at Agent Hansen, Jack displayed his still intact sense of humor. "Now I know how you get people to confess. They want to escape this wretched smell. Good God, how do you stand this day in and day out?"

Hansen smiled at last. "Ha, I don't even smell it anymore. Besides pine is preferable to the aroma of some of our alleged criminals." He led Jack and Mary to the rock-hard wooden chairs then walked to the other side to sit facing them. "Present company excluded. You two smell like sunscreen and sea breeze."

Mary rolled her eyes. "Thank you, Agent Hansen, but can we get this interview over with? We have a plane to catch."

"Then I'll get to the point. Jack, did you push Vern Bradley over the railing of the *Queen of the Seas*?"

Jack didn't blink as he stared straight into Hansen's eyes. "I don't know. I just don't know."

"What do you mean you don't know? Either you did or you didn't. What is it?"

"I admit I hit back after that bastard shoved me, but I don't know if he fell overboard," Jack answered.

"Are you telling me you couldn't see whether he fell. I see you wear glasses, but even the poorest of vision shouldn't stop you from seeing whether the man fell over the edge." Hansen's tone was gruff. "Did he fall or not?"

"I didn't see him fall because I tripped and landed face down on the deck. Got the concussion to prove it. The last time I saw Vern Bradley, he was wobbling on the edge of the railing, laughing at me. Then something caught my foot and I fell."

"Something just caught your foot? What do you think that might have been, Jack?"

"Are you mocking me?" Jack asked. "I don't know what the hell caught my foot. If I didn't think it sounded far-fetched, I'd say someone grabbed it from behind. It all happened so fast. I bounced off Vern's big, fat gut and the next thing I knew my foot came out from under me and I woke up with a terrible headache."

"It does sound a little far-fetched, to be honest. Is that the best you can do?" Agent Hansen had definitely changed his tune, Jack noted. No more mister nice guy.

Jack sat a little straighter and clenched his teeth. "I

can't do better because that's the truth. That's what you want, isn't it? Now, can we go catch our plane?"

"About that," Hansen said, "We can't let you leave the area, especially now that we have an eyewitness. And, yes, I want the truth, but your truth doesn't match with the eyewitness account I just heard."

Jack gasped. "I thought Vern and I were alone on that deck. Who saw us?"

"Sounds like you thought you could get away with this without getting caught." Hansen raised an eyebrow as he made eye contact with Jack. "Unfortunately, I'm not at liberty to give you names, but this person said they saw you push Vern Bradley over the edge."

Mary chimed in. "Where was this person when it happened? Why is this just now coming to light? My God, if someone saw the incident, they should have said something at the time."

"It is concerning that they waited, but it seems there was some trepidation about how this might affect family members. But in the end, they decided it was important to tell the truth."

"And you believe their truth over my truth?" Jack asked.

"They could both be true. You don't know if you pushed Vern over and this person says you definitely did. You didn't see the outcome, but it looks like we know the outcome now."

Jack thought about the possible eyewitness. It had to be Robert. That would explain his remarks as he left a few minutes ago.

"If the eyewitness is Mary's son, Robert, you should know he is not my biggest fan. He seems to think his mother should have stayed with Vern, abuse and all."

"I didn't say it was Robert."

"But you aren't denying it. That's enough for me," Jack said.

"Believe what you want. All I know is I have an eyewitness and because of that, I have to detain you on suspicion of murder."

"Detain me? What does that mean? Do I have to come back here and stand trial?" Jack knew there was a possibility it would come to this, but now he wondered how that might look.

"No, you won't have to come back. I'm afraid you won't be going back to Seattle for a while. In fact, we need to take you into custody."

"You're going to hold me on the word of one person?" Jack tried to stand up, but Mary took his hand and pulled him back down.

"I have no choice." Agent Hansen looked down at the table, avoiding the eyes of both Jack and Mary.

"Look at me, Jack." Mary touched his face and gently turned his cheek in her direction. "We got this, dear. There must be a way to get you out of custody." She set her steely gaze on Hansen and asked, "What do we need to do to get him out of here?"

Chapter Nineteen

A Comfortable Prison

Vern Bradley was stuck—stuck between a pile of dirty sweat socks and a bag of stale potato chips. At Carmen's insistence, Javier had sacrificed his room to keep Vern in this makeshift prison cell and from the conversation Vern overheard between mother and son, Javier was not happy about giving up his space. Carmen eventually got her way but listening to the lippy kid raise his voice to his mother made Vern's blood boil. Neither of his boys would dare talk back to him at the risk of a swift smack across their cheek—always with an open hand of course, leaving a temporary red mark but nothing the boys couldn't handle. Kids needed to know their place.

No, Vern did not like Javier's attitude, but he needed his help, so as soon as he heard Carmen leave for her date, he knocked from the inside of his prison door.

"Javier! Hey, kid, come let me out of here for a minute." No answer. Vern raised his voice and banged on the door again. "I know you're out there. Turn down the God damn TV and listen to me." The volume on the television went down slightly. "Javier?"

"I hear you, *señor*. Mama would kill me if I let you out."

"Good God, kid. I'm sixty-seven years old and

you're what? Twenty? Twenty-five? I'm no match for you. Just let me out so I can breathe some fresher air. Either that or come get your chips and sweat socks and get me a bottle of Pine Sol."

"Why should I help you? You took my room, and we haven't seen any money from your family."

"You'll get your money, but right now I need a glass for my Irish whiskey. Maybe you'd like to share it with me."

"You have enough to share? Mama locked the liquor cabinet and took the key, but she left the key to my room hanging on the kitchen wall. Maybe I could let you out for a few minutes."

"There you go. Get us a coupla glasses and we can share this bottle of Jameson." Vern heard the kid's bare feet slap the tile floor. The sound of the cupboard opening along with the clink of glassware led Vern to believe Javier was on board with the plan and within a minute the lock on the door clicked. Javier opened it slowly and as Vern poked his head out, he was greeted with a giant glass vase poised to crack his head open with one false move.

With hands raised, holding a wad of sweat socks in one hand and a bottle of Jameson in the other, Vern moved back a step. "Hey, buddy, I'm not gonna hurt you. I just want to get out of your stinky room."

Javier lowered the vase but kept his gaze on Vern. "All right, *señor*, you can come out, but no funny moves. I'll get some glasses." He backed into the kitchen taking his eyes off his target only to grab the two tumblers. "Go sit in the recliner where I can watch you."

Vern followed Javier's command taking slow steps to the brightly colored chair. As he sank into the soft cushion splattered with a turquoise, red, and yellow floral print, he knew he wouldn't easily find his way back up. Javier would surely feel safe with an old guy like him stuck in the comfy chair.

****

Lying on the soft white lounge chair on her balcony, Gladys watched the sun sink into the sea. Things hadn't turned out quite as expected, but retirement in the condo Vern paid for and the extra money she would soon see from his insurance policy would make life more than comfortable.

Comfortable... Is that what Glady really wanted? Despite his penchant for physical abuse, she had to admit she actually missed Vern. The truth was, he'd only abused Mary and the boys, saving his sweet side for Gladys. In thirty years, he'd never once laid a hand on her except to love her and she repaid him with an overdose of sleeping pills. What was she thinking? Maybe she thought she'd find a younger lover to pass the time, but after drooling over the building's handyman and feeling the heat coming off the pool boy, she wasn't sure she was up for the ride. Her money might buy her some fun, but is that what she really wanted?

Vern had always been a means to an end for Gladys—she slept with him, and he helped her live a more comfortable life. At first, all she hoped for was a little extra money to keep the creditors from her door. Vern not only gave her a little extra in her paycheck, he went out of his way to bring her groceries or pick up take-out food every time he stopped by to cash in on Gladys' sexual favors. He wasn't the greatest lover she'd had, but with a little coaching, he hit the mark most of the time. So, with Vern, her bills were paid, she wasn't going hungry, and she actually enjoyed his company both in and out of bed. He could be an asshole for sure, but he was funny and surprisingly smart. The arrangement was practical—perfect for a no-nonsense woman like Gladys, but somewhere along the way it seems she had fallen in love with the big lug. And now she was feeling just a little guilty about doctoring his whiskey with too many sleeping pills. Truthfully, she was glad it hadn't worked. She missed him.

Her thoughts were interrupted by a knock on her door...

****

It hadn't taken Vern long to get Javier stinking drunk. The boy was used to beer and cheap tequila, so when he got a taste of that good Irish whiskey, he dove into it like a man racing the clock. "One more, *señor*," he asked over and over again until his chin finally hit his chest as he passed out cold.

If I'd have known it would be this easy, I would have tried this sooner, Vern thought. As expected, it was a chore getting his sixty-seven-year-old ass out of the comfy chair, but with a couple of heave ho's he managed to stand. He'd only taken a couple sips of the whiskey after the first shot, so he was sober and ready to get the hell out of there.

Where was his phone? Could Carmen have left it in the house, and did he even have time to look for it? The *Queen of the Seas* was only in port until 8:00 p.m. and it was 7:15 p.m. now. Carmen's accomplice in Vern's escape had surely gotten his reward by now and would be dropping Carmen at her door any moment. He had to get the hell out and fast. With Javier plopped over face down on the couch, Vern saw his opportunity—Javier's phone poking out of his back pocket. Vern pulled it out causing the kid to stir.

"Whas goin on?" Javier mumbled then dropped his head right back down on the couch.

"It's a message from your mama. Your phone was buzzing so I grabbed it. But I can't get in without your password. Give it to me really quick and I'll get the message for you."

"Why should I tell you?"

"Because you're in no shape to answer and I wouldn't want to piss off your mama. I can help you here. Just give me your password and I'll send her a good answer."

Javier lifted his head and gave Vern a blank stare. "You're all right, man. Okay the password is mirandasi2si."

"Like the letter C or the ocean Sea?" Vern asked.

"Like *si señor*. *Si*, number 2, *si*. Pretty clever, huh?" Javier chuckled, then closed his eyes. "Don't tell my mama I've been drinking."

"My lips are sealed, kid. You can go back to sleep now."

Javier dropped his head and snorted, then eased into a steady snore. Yeah, his lips were sealed, but he wished he could see Carmen's face when she found him face down in a drunken stupor—and her prisoner long gone.

Vern tried the password in Javier's phone and found success. He looked for an Uber app and maybe an Apple Pay account. Neither came up, so he looked up the local taxi service, called them as he was heading to the door and asked them to pick him up a few blocks away. Carmen had taken his wallet, but he'd find a way to get this paid at his destination—the El Dorado condominiums. He ran out the door and headed to the pick-up spot away from town, so Carmen would not see him on her way back.

As the driver drove up, he jumped in, and they headed off.

****

Who could be at the door? Gladys opened the door and there he stood. "Vern!"

Chapter Twenty

Watch Out Gladys

"Hello, darlin'. Surprised to see me?" Vern patted Gladys' ass as he crossed the threshold of his condo. He'd paid for it, for God's sake, he had every right to march right in.

"Where have you been, dear?" Gladys' face looked like she'd seen a ghost, but her voice was light and cheery. Despite recent events, Vern had to admire her ability to absorb his icy stare without flinching.

"Recovering from too many sleeping pills in my whiskey. I see you tried to make my death legit, but we can do this without you literally killing me." He continued to stare, hoping to get her to come clean.

"What are you talking about? I just put your sleeping pill in your drink like I always do. I think I may have added an extra one since you were so stressed. Was it too much for you this time?" She didn't break eye contact, but her lashes fluttered as she blinked a little too quickly.

"You know what you did, and *I* know what you did, so let's just put it behind us and move on. I have no place else to go and we need to get this insurance claim settled." He tried not to smile. "But enough for pleasant conversation. I need some cash or your credit card to pay the cab driver. Why don't you go down and pay him while I go find something to drink. I'll be making my own drinks from now on, by the way."

"Sure, Vern. I'll go pay. Make yourself comfortable." She smiled.

****

Gladys looked over her shoulder as she walked out the door. Was her smile convincing? Did Vern believe she was happy to see him? She paced in front of the elevator, wondering if Vern would follow her. As the elevator door closed, she let it out.

"Shit!" Her voice pushed out a sigh with the words. "He's alive and he knows what I did." Thoughts of his retribution filled her head—would he start beating on her like he did Mary and the boys? Would he go for the ultimate payback and try to kill her? Vern was a hard man to read. Even after thirty years she still didn't know what would set him off. Would he forgive her, or would this be the end?

The elevator door opened interrupting her downward spiraling thoughts—for the moment, anyway. She had to pay the taxi driver, then she would go back upstairs and pretend like everything was fine. And maybe it would be fine. She had to admit, she was relieved that she hadn't succeeded in her murder attempt. Over the past few days, she found that she missed the old bugger. Maybe they could start fresh.

Gladys walked out to the parking lot and paid the taxi driver, giving him a big tip. This nice young man had brought her man back to her and she would do her best to make up for her one mistake. Vern would be upstairs waiting for her, and she was ready for the reunion.

Riding back up to the fifth floor, her thoughts had turned to the physical side of her reunion with Vern. If she could get him into bed immediately, he would soften. She was well aware that, even at age sixty, she still had the power to tame her own personal beast. The benefits she would reap were incidental, but she was looking forward to relieving a little sexual tension in the process. The thought brought a smile to her face as she navigated the short walk down the hallway to her new life.

As she turned the key, the door swung open.

"Welcome back, darlin'." Vern's smile didn't match his words. Something told Gladys he was not quite ready to forgive and forget.

"I've missed you," Gladys cooed, her words sounding more like a purring kitten than her normal "no-nonsense" tone. "Why don't you come with me and check out our new bedroom."

Vern's eyes started at the top, taking in her blonde/gray hair—a bit mussed from a recent nap on the balcony—and her blue eyes sparkling despite the lack of eye makeup. She watched as his eyes moved down to her still perky breasts peeking out of her peacock-blue halter top. He didn't rest there too long as his favorite body part had always been her ass and shapely legs, which were conveniently extending from a pair of tight white shorts. Gladys watched his eyes glaze over and knew she had him.

Pulling his face down to her level as she wrapped her arms around his neck, she kissed him, at first gently, then more fervently as she jumped up and wrapped her legs around his ample body. Grabbing his favorite butt cheeks, he pulled his lips away long enough to ask, "Which way to our playground, darlin'?"

"Second door on the right," Gladys said as she pointed down the hallway. She buried her head in the chest hair that seemed to sprout from his flowered shirt. In a few minutes she'd be getting the ride she'd been missing.

****

Gladys threw her head back let out a squeal. "Oh, Vern, you outdid yourself tonight." She was enjoying her perch on top of her man.

"And you outdid yourself last week when you doctored my whiskey. If you weren't such a fine piece of ass, I'd have had you arrested." Vern pushed her off his lap and sat up.

"You don't mean that, do you?" Gladys asked as she rolled to the edge of the bed. "You know I didn't overdose you on purpose. You do know that don't you?"

"That was way too much for an accident, darlin'. Lucky for you I'm a forgiving man, not to mention I can't show my face to the cops if we ever hope to cash in on my insurance policy." He flashed her a toothy smile as his eyes narrowed.

Would he really forgive her, Gladys wondered? She touched his cheek silently thanking him although his eyes didn't seem to match his brilliant smile. "Are you all right? Do you really forgive me for my... er...mistake?"

He pulled her hand from his face, holding her wrist in a vise grip. "I'll forgive you, darlin', but I won't forget." He tightened his grip causing Gladys to wince.

"You're hurting me."

Staring into her eyes, but not letting loose, he said, "I know."

"Then, stop. Please, Vern, let go of me."

Vern laughed as he let go of her wrist and slapped her hand away. "Sorry. I didn't mean to hold on so tight—it was an accident."

Gladys jumped out of bed, pulled on her robe, and started to walk toward the kitchen. "Can I get you anything, dear?"

Vern's smile faded. "As I said before, I'll make my own drinks. I'm right behind you."

With the TV off and no music in the room, Gladys was startled when her phone's ringtone cut through the silence. She grabbed the phone as Vern was walking toward her and pressed answer without looking to see who was calling.

"Hello?"

"Hi, Mom." Darlene said. "Do you have a minute to talk?"

Gladys looked at Vern and wondered if she was safe. "Yeah, honey, I've got all the time in the world."

Chapter Twenty-One

Pre-trial Release

Mary was not about to let her man spend a night in custody, a position she made very clear to Special Agent Hansen. All the family members had been interviewed by early afternoon and Hansen was about to schedule a pre-trial release hearing for the next day. Mary was having none of it.

"There are still plenty of hours in this day, Agent Hansen, and I don't want to leave my sixty-nine-year-old husband in a cold jail cell for even one night." Mary seemed to have taken Hansen's gaze hostage, her green eyes daring him to look away. "Jack took a pretty bad fall thanks to my ex-husband. If you're going to lock him up, you damn well better put me in there with him. I won't leave him alone."

"Let me see what I can do about getting an emergency hearing." Hansen had a heart after all, Mary thought. "Do you have an attorney?" he asked.

"We'll have one. My son, Sam, is pretty well-connected in this area. I'm sure he can find someone in a hurry." Mary stood up and headed for the door, looking back at Jack. She turned to face Agent Hansen and asked, "Can you wait to lock him up?"

"He can sit out front with the family for now. We've got a guard at the door." Hansen cracked the tiniest hint of a smile. "As I said before, I don't think he's a flight risk."

Mary turned to Jack. Did she see the tear rolling down his cheek? "Jack, didn't you hear Agent Hansen? You don't have to go to some jail cell. You can sit here and talk to your daughter while Sam and I track down a lawyer for you. Please give me a smile, dear."

Jack blinked and gave her a half-assed smile. "I hate feeling my sixty-nine-year-old body marks me as a pathetic old man, too slow to escape. I'd like to show them all I'm a threat, a flight risk as Hansen said in his God damn condescending tone. I bet I could outrun those guys at the door, and I'd do it right now...if it weren't for their guns." He closed his eyes and hung his head. "You go talk to Sam, I'll be a good boy and sit quietly."

****

Jack regretted using his sarcastic tone when he spoke to Mary at FBI headquarters. He wanted to be the strong one and take control of the situation, but Mary had taken the reins and with Sam's help, she fixed everything. How could he not love her for taking care of him in his time of need? Her strength and independence were the qualities he loved most, but he felt so useless right now. He made this mess; he should have cleaned it up. Was he really getting too old to take care of himself?

The past eight hours had pulled every emotion out of Jack's normally stoic persona. Fear arrived first like a sharp punch to his gut as he faced the interrogation, his erratic heartbeat and sweaty palms ramping up the feeling of dread. After that was over, he couldn't help feeling a tinge of resentment as Mary and Sam were so easily able to secure an attorney and push for an immediate hearing. Not only did Jack feel guilty for disrupting everyone's life, but he also felt inadequate. While he was feeling sorry for himself, Mary and Sam took on the challenge and within an hour William Fuller, Jr., Attorney at Law, arrived to take on Jack's case. Jack's fear had returned when he looked into the bright blue eyes of this very young, obviously green, lawyer. A few hours later, however, after a lengthy consultation and the pre-trial hearing Agent Hansen had arranged, Jack's fear had turned to gratitude. Young Will Fuller may have been green, but what he lacked in experience, he made up for with knowledge and a confident demeanor. A few minutes in front of the judge bought Jack a conditional pre-trial release—Jack would not be allowed to leave the area, but due to the advanced age of the defendant (Jack had cringed when he heard that argument), the trial would take place in two months.

Now, sitting on the soft gray sofa in Justin's San Francisco condo with Mary by his side, he felt pure joy. Yes, it had been an emotional day, but he was safe now and he was with his beautiful new wife. Justin and Annie had volunteered their extra bedroom for the next two months so he would take this time, maybe his last bit of freedom, to enjoy his family.

"Can I get you more hot chocolate, Grandpa Jack?" Annie asked. "I know it's the middle of summer, but compared to the Mexican heat, it feels chilly here."

Jack felt that chill, deep in his bones and even deeper in his heart. "Sure, Annie, I could use a warm-up." If only hot chocolate could warm his soul.

"How about you, Mary? Do you—" Annie stopped mid-sentence and whispered to Jack. "Looks like your bride nodded off."

"She can sleep through my snoring, so I don't think

you'll wake her." He touched the soft red curls falling on his shoulder, then moved his hand to her beautiful face. "She's had a hell of a day, so I'm not about to move her."

"I'll get you that warm-up and let you two sit out here for a while. You know where your room is when you're ready for bed." Annie took his cup and headed for the kitchen.

Jack sat silently, leaning into Mary, their heads resting on one another as their hearts beat in perfect sync.

****

When Annie came out with the hot chocolate, Jack and Mary were fast asleep, still sitting upright wrapped in one another's arms. As she was placing the comforter across their laps, Justin emerged from his favorite chair in the corner of the room. He often sat there working on his laptop—it seemed his work was never done. Tonight, he'd been sitting in the dimly lit living room and as the conversation with Jack and Mary had dwindled, he stopped to admire the view of the city.

Justin turned to look at Annie. "We're lucky to be here."

"It's not luck that you're so smart, babe. You and I worked hard for this and just maybe we had a little luck finding just the right job at the right place." Annie took the few steps between the couch and Justin's chair, moved his computer from his lap to the nearby table, and replaced it with her warm body. She wrapped her arms around his neck.

Justin's arms encircled her as he kissed her, a gentle kiss that made her shiver. "I never dreamed I'd be looking at the skyline of San Francisco from our own condo." Justin said. "But as much as I love our home, I think my luck has more to do with finding you."

"You know I feel the same. Love you, Justie." Annie snuggled into her love. "Now we need to make sure those two on the couch get some of our good luck."

"I know my grandpa is innocent. There isn't a mean bone in his body."

"I hope the jury feels the same." Annie sighed. "I want everything to go back to normal, so we can plan our wedding day. I'd really like it to be as soon as possible."

"I've asked you a thousand times and you said you didn't need to be married. What changed?" Justin asked.

"Those two lovebirds dozing on the couch. I want us to be just like them."

Chapter Twenty-Two

Back in Seattle

Darlene had barely spoken to Robert on the trip home to Seattle. No sense creating a scene on the airplane and, frankly, she just didn't want to talk to him. Yes, she wanted the insurance money from Vern's apparent demise—she wasn't above the scam faking his death—but was it really necessary for Robert to claim to be an eyewitness? They could get Jack convicted on circumstantial evidence without committing perjury. And maybe Jack could even plead self-defense. They didn't need to see him fry to get the money.

Now as they walked into their home overlooking Puget Sound, she dropped her carry-on bag with an audible sigh.

"Don't be so dramatic. Save your heavy breathing for the bedroom," Robert said. "Why are you so pissed off, anyway?"

"You know very well why I'm pissed." Leaving her bag in the entryway, she moved to the kitchen to find a bottle of her favorite wine. She worked the corkscrew with ease—she'd done this a thousand times—opening the bottle, then taking a few steps to the cupboard holding the wine glasses. She was tempted to put the bottle directly to her lips and forget the damn glass.

"You women always think we can read your fucking

minds." Robert headed to the liquor cabinet, retrieving a bottle of Jack Daniels. "What did I do to bring on the deep freeze?"

"I'm worried about you. You told the FBI agent your saw Jack push Vern over the edge. Jack could go to jail for life with just your word." Darlene took a swig of the heavy pour of wine she'd prepared. "I want the money as bad as you, but I'm sure we could have gotten it with a self-defense plea or manslaughter at worst, but you're sentencing him to death in prison if he's charged with murder."

"Why do you care what happens to Jack?" Robert said as he found a glass to hold his precious bourbon. "I thought you were on board with this."

"I'm on board with getting an insurance settlement for an accident at sea, but even I'm not cold enough to want Jack to suffer in prison." She leaned against the kitchen counter as she watched Robert swallow a mouthful of bourbon. "I think the thing that bothers me the most is realizing that you *are* that cold."

"I've had to be cold to get along in this world. You know that. My father beat me as a kid and now I'm going to cash in by faking his death. Sometimes I wish it had actually happened."

"And yet you seem to want to punish the only person who tried to shield you from him—your mother. If you take Jack away from her, she'll never forgive you."

"You said the magic word, she *tried* to shield me, but she couldn't. We both suffered at my dad's hand." Robert ran his fingers through his mop of dark hair and turned his eyes to the floor.

"Can't you even look at me, Bobby? What's with you? One minute you defend your father, and the next minute cry about his abuse. Which is it?" She walked to him and pushed on his chin until his eyes could no longer avoid her gaze. "Why are you punishing your mother for the sins of your father?"

Darlene studied his sky-blue eyes. Had that sadness always been there? He tried to avert his gaze, but she saw the tears forming as he spoke. "I hate both of my parents—my dad for using his fucking belt as a weapon and my mom for letting him get away with it. Why didn't she take us away from him?" He pounded his glass on the counter. "But if she'd done that, I wouldn't have learned the business and I wouldn't have met you." He pulled her hand from his chin and pulled her close. "I just want both of my parents out of my life, a couple million dollars, and you in my bed 24/7. If I have to lie to get that, I'll do it."

"I want to be with you, too, but you gotta pull back that eyewitness testimony. You could go to prison and then where would we be?"

"I'm sorry, baby. I'll tell my truth when we get to trial."

"And what exactly is *your* truth?" She touched his cheek. "You can tell me."

"I've told you. Dad didn't fall over. You know that, but it's not because Jack didn't try. He rammed into Dad's big beer gut and bounced back, kind of in a daze it seemed. As my old man was teetering on the edge, Jack regained his footing and was lurching forward to deliver the final blow. If I hadn't run out and grabbed Jack's ankle, he would have killed my dad." Robert's voice had escalated to a fever pitch, but now his voice softened. "He would have killed him, I swear."

"But he didn't," Darlene said, turning her eyes away

from Robert.

"Why are you suddenly so moralistic, babe? Don't you want the money?" Robert grabbed her face with both hands, compelling her to meet his eyes.

"I do, but now that I've met Jack, I hate to see him go to jail. Can't we just say it was self-defense, or an accident? Why are you so set on seeing Jack fry?"

"You're acting like Jack is your fucking father. My dad was more of a father to you." He dropped his hands, but she continued to look upward.

"All Vern ever did was bring me trinkets so he could keep me occupied while he fucked my mom. Jack is more like the dad I wished I'd have had—and your mom deserves to be happy."

"My mom did nothing to protect me from my dad. Jack is just a casualty of her guilt." Robert's voice was flat and devoid of emotion and Darlene shivered with the chill of his words. "Can't be avoided. We need him to go down."

****

Darlene had said nothing at the finality of Robert's words—he'd made up his mind and there was nothing she could do to alter his misguided scheme. With a turn of her heel, she'd taken her full glass of wine into the bedroom, hoping for a few moments alone. Robert knew the signal and left her alone for the required interval of time—an unspoken cooling off period they both seemed to agree was about thirty minutes. And as usual, once she downed the wine, she was less averse to Robert's presence. Damn him, anyway, she thought as he entered their bedroom and she succumbed to his sexual touch.

Now, lying next to him, she wondered if she'd hitched her wagon to the wrong star when she chose to travel through life with Robert. The potential for money and great sex had drawn her in a few years ago when they finally connected, but now that she was dodging his moody temper outbursts at every turn, she wondered if it was really worth it? Soon they'd have more money, but would she have to lie under oath to make that happen? Would Robert get caught in his lies? The complications were adding up day by day leaving her wishing for a nurturing presence.

Robert usually lashed out at her when she expressed her fears, and her mother—so far away now—was anything but nurturing. So, she lay in silence on her soft silk sheets next to Robert wrapped in a blanket of anxiety. Usually, a good orgasm would calm her, but tonight it had just revved up her senses while it had sent Robert directly to sleep. His heavy breath kept erupting in a snort every few minutes, sending her closer to the edge.

"Bobby, wake up!" She rolled toward him and pushed on his shoulder. "Roll over, Bobby. You're snoring." When he failed to move, she pushed again. No luck. Just another, somewhat louder, snort. "Damn you. Must be nice to live without guilt."

Darlene sat up, her anxiety ramping up with each annoying snort. Reaching for her phone on the night table, she tapped on the number of Gladys Dunwoody. She needed to talk to her mommy.

****

The phone call from Darlene was a welcome respite from Vern's accusations. Gladys tried to distance herself from the man, but he followed her through the living room and out onto the balcony.

"What do you mean you have all the time in the

world?" Darlene asked.

"Oh, nothing. I just missed you and I'd like to talk awhile if you have the time." Gladys winced as Vern grabbed her arm. His eyes bore into hers as she showed no sign of ending her conversation with her daughter. Tightening his hold, Vern put the forefinger of his other hand to his lips and whispered, "Shhhh." Why didn't he want Darlene to know he was there?

"Are you okay, Mom? Do you really miss me?"

"I'm fine, dear." Gladys inhaled to weather the pain of Vern's vise-like grip.

"You seem distracted. Is someone there?" Darlene asked.

"No, of course not," Gladys lied. "I'm all alone, as usual. Why wouldn't I be?"

"Is that the reason you want a long conversation with me? You're lonely? I can't remember the last time we had a heart-to-heart conversation—did we ever have that kind of talk? I mean, I'm glad you want to talk to me, but I'm surprised."

"Oh, honey, I always have time for my little girl. I really miss you. How are you and Robert doing?"

"That's why I wanted to talk to you. Mom, I think Vern is still alive and Robert is going to testify that he saw Jack push him overboard."

"Oh dear, that might get him in a lot of trouble if Vern surfaces." Gladys glared at Vern as she pulled her arm from his grasp. "If he's still alive, let's hope he stays out of sight."

"This must be hard for you, Mom. Do you still love him?"

Gladys seized the opportunity to reel Vern back in. "Of course, I do, dear. I love that man with all my heart.

He's my soulmate," she cooed. Smiling at Vern as she spewed the syrupy sweet words, she knew she had him. "I miss him so much, honey. I hope he turns up soon."

Gladys knew she had appeased Vern with her words and was relieved to see him smile, even if it looked a bit smug. How was she going to convince him she was back in the saddle and under his perceived control? Submission was not Gladys' strong suit, in fact, Vern might not recognize her if she played the obedience card, so balancing her kick-ass personality with an ounce or two of deference would be a challenge.

"Mom, don't you think he's still alive? I can't help thinking those texts from his phone are for real. I don't think someone would sneak him off the ship and then kill him. He's got to be alive."

"Honey, we just have to proceed as if he were dead. That's the only way we'll get the money. I don't want to know the truth," Gladys lied.

"Honestly, I hope he is dead. He's really done a number on Robert." Darlene sighed.

"I hear you, honey. It would be better for all of us." Gladys glared at Vern, hoping he hadn't heard the other side of the conversation. "Much better."

Chapter Twenty-Three

Carmen Pays the Price

Carmen had been prepared to pay for Harold Stein's manipulation of ship's records with her body. He wasn't a bad looking guy—he might have even caught her eye if his shirt hadn't been buttoned up to the top button and his thick glasses hadn't obscured his possibly handsome face—he was just not the kind of guy women noticed. But Carmen knew she owed him for Vern's undetected exit from the *Queen of the Seas*. What's a quick fuck in the grand scheme of things when looking at a $200,000 payoff?

What she didn't account for was making her flesh donation this soon. It was only Friday and the ship hit Puerto Vallarta every Monday, but Harold had jumped ship last Monday—just for the week he later told her— and it seemed he was hoping to cash in on his date with Carmen sooner rather than later. It had taken him until Wednesday to call her and the tremor she heard in his voice caused Carmen to wonder if he would suffer performance anxiety. No matter, she just wanted to get it over with and wasn't expecting the normal niceties of a first date. Was it actually a date, after all? Or just payback? That question had been answered when Harold arrived at her door with a bouquet of red roses.

Date or not, he still expected sex and Carmen knew

it. The Uber delivered them to the Sheraton near the ship where Harold ushered Carmen to a room overlooking the Marina. Hoping to move things along, she had dropped her purse on the bedside table and began unbuttoning her blouse.

"Stop." Harold's voice was gentle. "I've been waiting for a long time for this moment, and I don't want it just because you feel obligated. Let's have a glass of wine and sit on the balcony." He had taken her hand and led her to the small outside table where two wine glasses sat waiting to be filled with what looked like a very expensive cabernet. Between them, a shrimp cocktail with two forks lay imbedded in ice surrounded by chocolate covered strawberries.

Carmen had never been attracted to Harold. He was her friend, nothing more, but this gesture made it easier to take the next step. When the last strawberry passed her lips, Harold took her hand once again, seemingly bolstered by the liquid courage contained in two glasses of wine, and led her to the bed. His hands were shaking so Carmen took the lead, unbuttoning her own blouse as she slipped out of her sandals and skirt. Was he that shy? It seemed so as he turned away to remove his clothing and set his glasses on the closest side table.

Without the button choking shirt and the thick black rimmed glasses, Harold wasn't half bad, his dark hair framing his tanned face and his deep brown eyes almost sexy surrounded by long dark lashes. And...from the waist down he definitely exceeded expectations. But did he know what to do with it? Carmen had been expecting to hold her breath during the ordeal and take it like a dose of bitter medicine. But a dose of Harold Stein had proved to be anything but bitter. All the years she had avoided his numerous attempts to secure just one date with her, she cursed the time she'd wasted searching for a more passionate man. There clearly was not a more passionate man than Harold and after paying for his favor with her flesh, she now hoped to keep paying.

A few hours later as she rode home in the Uber, she smiled thinking of how she would spend every Monday when *The Queen of the Seas* stopped in Puerto Vallarta.

****

Carmen's afterglow faded quickly when she opened the door to her condo. Javier was lying face down on the couch, the coffee table littered with chips, shot glasses, and an almost empty bottle of Jameson Irish whiskey. That wouldn't have been much of surprise by itself, but when she saw the door to his room ajar—the room that was supposed to be holding Vern—she feared the worst. Javier's snores propelled his whiskey breath through the air, producing a stench that made Carmen madder by the minute. Shaking his shoulder as she passed by the couch on the way to the open room, she struggled to get his attention…without success. Marching toward the open bedroom door, she got the answer she expected. Vern was gone.

"Damn you!" She yelled loud enough to wake the dead, but not loud enough to get a rise out of Javier. With a sharp turn and quick steps, she was in his face and pulled his head up by his long black hair. He coughed and rolled his eyes. "Wake up, damn it. What's going on? Where the hell is Vern?"

Javier swallowed, his words tripping over his thick tongue. "He was right here jus' a minute ago. Dint you get his text?"

"Why would he be texting me?" Carmen asked. "I

have his phone."

"He was helping me answer you on my phone." Javier slurred the words.

"I didn't text you. Where is your phone?"

Javier pushed himself to a half-assed sitting position and reached in his pocket. "Oh shit. It's not here." He leaned over to check the floor and fell on the coffee table.

Carmen grabbed his hair again. "You drunken fool. You let him get away and it seems he took your phone. Not only did we lose out on a big payday, you lost your phone. You're on your own this time, buddy. I'm not buying you a new phone."

"He was so nice to me," Javier said as he held his head in his hands. "He prolly jus' went to get some beer."

Carmen rolled her eyes as she stared at her son. "You didn't get your brains from me, did you, Javier? Why would he come back to be held hostage? He's free now and we have no idea where to find him."

"Mama, I may be drunk, but I can find him." Javier smiled, his eyes half closed.

"It is a big city. Why do you think you can find this man?" Carmen's voice had raised to a higher pitch. "We will never see a dime if we lose track of him."

"I got this, Mama. I got…" Javier's voice trailed off as his head fell back.

Carmen shook her head and walked away. No sense trying to reason with her drunk-ass kid. How had he sunk so low? He hadn't had much of a father figure in his life, but she'd done her best to give him all he needed, working a second job in the summer to supplement her teacher's salary. And now her freeloading son had ruined her chance to catch a break—or had he? Pulling her phone from her purse, she tapped on Javier's name in her contact. Hopefully, Vern would answer her call.

****

Vern felt the vibration of Javier's phone in the pocket of his shorts as the mariachi band ring tone announced the call. Backing away from Gladys, who was ending her call with Darlene, he moved quickly so she wouldn't hear the annoying music in the background. As he made his way to the balcony, he pulled the phone from his pocket to see a picture of Carmen and the word Mama on the screen. Hesitating for only a moment, he decided to take the call.

"Well, if it isn't my captor," Vern said with a smile. "Looks like you're out of a payday."

"Oh, I'm not so sure about that," Carmen said. "If I tell the Policia you are alive, no one will get paid. I think you might want to pay me for my silence."

"Why would I do that?" Vern asked. "No one saw me leave the ship, thanks to your friend tampering with the computer system. I believe that's a crime, darlin'. And if you should convince them I'm alive, I'd have to have you arrested for kidnapping and holding me hostage." Vern laughed. "I don't think you want to put you and your friend in jeopardy."

"It might be worth it to see your greedy family end up with nothing." Carmen's voice was escalating in both pitch and volume as she continued. "And you are the worst. I saved your life, and this is how you repay me? To think I felt sorry for your pathetic half-dead ass."

"I guess I didn't thank you properly, dear. Consider yourself thanked." Vern leaned against the railing as he watched Gladys glide onto the balcony parking the body he could never resist on the plush white lounge chair. He winked at her as he listened to Carmen.

Carmen did not seem to be backing down. "*Señor* Vern, Javier says he knows where you are, so don't get too comfortable."

"How does he know where I am? I didn't tell him where I was going. You will never find me. I have an entirely new identity and no one knows my name here."

"We will see about that." Carmen said. "I will let you go for now, but I will find you somehow. I am not going to let this opportunity pass me by—you owe me for your life."

"I think you're just shit out of luck, sister. I'm not paying you a dime." With that Vern pressed the button to end the call and looked at Gladys. "Guess I told her."

"Yes, Vern, you certainly did."

****

"Javier, wake up!" Carmen stood over her son speaking more softly this time, but it was enough to cause his eyes to pop open. From his angle, she must have looked much larger than her petite five-foot frame.

"Mama?" He cowered. "Please don't be mad at me."

"I will decide if I am mad after you tell me how you plan to find *Señor* Vern."

"Oh, that's easy. Give me your phone. There's an app called 'Find My Phone'. When I punch in my number it will give me the address of my phone." He was drunk but not so drunk he couldn't type his own number in. "There you go, Mama."

And there it was. Javier's phone had found its way to an address a few miles down the road. Now what?

Chapter Twenty-Four

The Wrong Son

Sam hadn't spoken to his father in over two years—not since his mom finally divorced the bastard. He had no desire to be nice to the man who abused his mother, his brother, Robert, and himself. So, when his phone lit up and he saw the name Vern Bradley flash on the screen, he knew nothing good could come of it. He answered anyway…

"Dad?" As much as Sam hated his father, he didn't wish him dead and a small part of him wanted to hear an apology even if it was forty years too late. Under the circumstances he was relieved to see he was alive not only because of the twinge of emotion he still felt for the man, but because now he knew Jack had not pushed him over. "You're alive!"

The female voice on the other end did not confirm Sam's statement. Far from it. Had someone stolen Vern's phone? His father was not on the other end of this call, but he listened.

"Do we really need to go over that again?" The woman said. "I'm waiting for my money. It's time for you to pay the $50,000 you owe me."

"For what?" Sam asked. "Who are you and where's my dad?"

"We texted about this. You know what to do,

Robert."

"Robert? You got the wrong son, lady. This is Sam. But please tell me what you and Robert have cooked up. Why does he owe you $50,000?"

The woman cleared her throat, rather audibly. What was her story? Sam wondered as he waited to hear what she had to say.

"Did I say $50,000? That was a little joke with Robert. I told him I would return his father's valuables— there is a diamond encrusted ring and a few gold chains in his suitcase I thought might be worth something and to be honest, I thought you'd be happy to pay to get these things back."

"So, you're saying once my father went missing, the ship just let you clean out his room and call us to return his stuff?" Sam could not believe security was so lax on the *Queen of the Seas*. But then again, maybe he could. The cruise had been touted as a luxury cruise but when it came right down to it, most of the amenities were second rate and the onboard investigation of Vern's disappearance was less than thorough. He wondered how many other passengers had fallen overboard.

"I guess it was wrong to arrange this return of valuables on my own, but if I didn't do it, they would not survive the lost and found. Believe me, I am doing you a favor."

"Frankly, I don't give a damn about my dad's stuff, but shouldn't you leave his room intact until the FBI checks the scene for evidence?" Sam asked. "What's your hurry?"

"We need to clean out this room for the next sailing. As head of housekeeping, I have been entrusted with this task. Security has cleared me to pack up his belongings and return them to the family."

"What did you say your name was? We will definitely need to get in touch with you when my father-in-law goes to trial. Why don't you give me your name and address and I'll pass it along to our attorney. And of course, I'll give it to Robert—I'm sure he'll be happy to pay you."

"Thank you, but I'll contact Robert myself."

The phone went dead.

****

Sam withdrew the phone from his ear, stared at the blank screen for a moment then fixed his gaze on Jamie who was curled up with her book on the other end of the couch. "That was weird," he said.

Jamie had long since dropped her novel and had been staring at Sam throughout the conversation, her eyes wide with questions. "Weird?" Jamie asked. "Sounded more like a crime in the making from this end. Who was that?"

"Some woman who says she's the head of housekeeping wanting $50,000 for us to buy back my dad's stuff."

"Can we check on her credentials? If the ship won't release anything to us, Dad's lawyer could probably get that information. Do you think she's for real?"

"I don't know, but I do know she got very nervous when she found out I wasn't Robert. My brother is definitely up to something."

"Why doesn't that surprise me? I can't believe you and Robert grew up in the same house with the same dysfunction and turned out so different."

"I don't believe it myself sometimes. We were so close when we were kids, protecting each other from

Dad's wrath. I don't know why things changed between us or how he ended up forgiving our dad. I don't think I can ever forgive that man for how he treated his family, especially my mom."

Jamie uncurled her legs and scooted toward Sam. Leaning into her husband, she wrapped her arms around him. "I'm so glad you survived your childhood and turned that negative energy around. While Robert held onto it, you left it behind and became such a kind, loving man. I feel so lucky that you chose to spend your life with me."

"I'm the lucky one." Sam cupped her chin in his hand and kissed her. "We'll get through this. We've just got to get your dad acquitted. Or should I say our dad. I think of him as my dad now, too. I love that man."

"He loves you, too. And so do I."

****

Robert was used to getting texts from his dad's phone, but now there was a call coming through. Either his father recovered his phone or he was about to talk to the person who was blackmailing him. After his confrontation with Darlene, he was in no mood for more complications. Hoping for some good news, he answered.

"Hello? Is it really you, Dad?"

"I'm afraid not. It is your father's savior. You do know I saved his life, don't you?"

Robert was surprised to hear a woman's voice. It had never been clear who was holding his father hostage. "You saved him? I would call it kidnapping, lady."

"Hardly. He was unconscious when I went in to turn down the sheets. He would have died if I hadn't intervened." She paused. "I know this is inconvenient for

170

someone who wants to collect on his death, so I'm asking you once again to pay me the $200,000 your father promised for my silence."

"I don't have that kind of money." Robert said through gritted teeth.

"But you will have more than enough when the insurance pays. If you can't come up with all of it, I'll settle for $50,000 now and the rest when you get the settlement."

"Let me speak to my dad to make sure you're telling me the truth. Is he really alive?"

"You will just have to believe me. I cannot unlock the door when I am here alone. Your father will try to escape."

"So, you admit you're holding him against his will."

"Only until I get the money he promised for my good deed. Are you not happy that I saved your father's life?"

Robert thought about her statement. Was he happy that Vern had survived? Would his life have been better without the old bastard? Probably. He might not have had the business success he found in his dad's company, but he might have had more peace of mind. He felt his throat tighten as he answered.

"I guess I would have to say I'm glad he is alive. I will pay you $50,000 if you give me your name and address."

"Make the payment out to Carmen Miranda and I will text you my bank information. If I don't see the money in five days, I will let the authorities know he is alive."

"And if you let the authorities know he's alive, I'll have you arrested for kidnapping. I don't think either one of us want to jeopardize that insurance payout."

"I'll be waiting for my money." Carmen said as she ended the call.

Robert had no intention of paying that woman. What would she do? She would end up in prison for holding his dad hostage if she revealed the truth. No, he was pretty sure this bitch would not come forward and he wasn't going to throw money at the problem. At least now he knew who he was dealing with, some dumb housekeeper. He'd ignore her for now. What could go wrong?

Chapter Twenty-Five

Acts of Conscience

What am I doing? Carmen thought. *I've never done a dishonest thing in my life and now I'm blackmailing this family for my silence.* Throughout her forty-five years, Carmen Miranda had followed every rule. No trips to the principal's office as a kid, no sneaking behind her parents' back as a teenager, no speeding tickets as an adult. She'd taken pride in her honesty even when it hadn't served her best interests. So how had she let Vern Bradley turn her into a scheming, blackmailing liar?

Carmen sank into the cushion recently crushed by Vern's bulkier mass. "Javier, will you give me the address where you found your phone?"

"Why, Mama?" Javier asked, still laying on the couch.

"I want to report Vern's location to the police."

Javier was wide awake now and sat upright—as upright as a drunk could be expected to sit. "Mama, you cannot do that. If they find he is alive, there is no money for us."

"I know. But I cannot keep up this lie."

"Please, Mama. We could use that money."

Carmen rose from her sunken cushion and moved to the couch, wrapping her arm around her son. "You are right. We could use the money, but if you stop drinking you could find a decent job and I would not have to work so hard to support the two of us."

Javier hung his head. "You wouldn't have to work so hard if we scored that $200,000. Life would be so much easier."

Carmen lifted his chin and looked in his glassy eyes. "Easier would be nice, but I need to be honest. I cannot do this."

"Then I will give you the address, but can you just wait a few weeks to think about this?" Javier asked.

"I guess there is no harm in waiting. I deserve a reward for saving that bastard's life. If they pay me, I will accept it as a reward, then I will report Mr. Vern's location."

****

Darlene quit following the rules at a young age, opting to deceive, coerce, and manipulate those around her for her own gain. Tantrums garnered attention when she was five, tears worked at age ten and by age fifteen she used both to get her way with the boys. Why not? She'd learned from her mother, Gladys Dunwoody, that men were easily pliable and playable. Over twenty years later, she was still scheming.

Using her feminine wiles on Robert had given her a very comfortable life—a decent salary, a handsome and proficient lover, and a few extra bucks she skimmed off the books. In case things didn't work out with Robert, she'd have a nice nest egg to hold her over till she found her next man. She hoped it wouldn't come to that as she had inadvertently fallen in love with Robert and wanted nothing more than to quit playing games and enjoy her life.

But this scheme to collect the life insurance money

by convicting an innocent man of murder was too much. No one had ever gotten hurt by her actions in the past, but Jack Madison would go to prison—probably for life—if they wanted to collect on the life insurance. She couldn't go through with it. After all these years, Darlene Dunwoody had developed a conscience.

****

Robert hadn't always been a schemer. He had been a good kid smothered with love by his mother and threatened with bodily harm by his father. Hard to say which kept him on the straight and narrow in those formative years as he lived with an angel on one shoulder and the devil on the other. Despite the pain of his father's corporal punishment, the devil eventually won the battle and Robert now lived in his father's shadow. Instead of turning from him, he chose to follow in his footsteps, anger ruling his decisions on a daily basis.

Robert, like his father, was ruled by money and he didn't care how he got it. If his dad was dead or alive, it didn't really matter to him. When the trial for Jack presented the opportunity for five million bucks, he would not hesitate to swear on a stack of bibles that he saw Jack Madison push his father over the railing of the *Queen of the Seas.*

Robert was not about to let his conscience get in his way.

****

If Gladys ever had a conscience, it was long gone. Life hadn't always been kind to her, in fact, between her childhood and her marriage to Darlene's no-good father, life had pretty much kicked her ass. So, when she landed at Bradley & Sons, she chose to kick life back—Gladys would take care of Gladys and whoever got in her way better watch out. And now, sitting in her condo, she knew she'd made the right choices. All the conniving, deception, and embezzling had landed her on easy street, but there was one obstacle lying naked in her bed—Vern Bradley. All she wanted was a nice quiet retirement—alone—on the beach and he had just ruined that dream. She needed to find a way to get him out of her life. Her conniving gene was still working overtime, so maybe it would be easier than she thought. Luckily, Gladys lost her conscience long ago.

Chapter Twenty-Six

Two Months Later

Every night, Jack looked forward to the moment Mary let her hair down and settled her sexy, sixty-five-year-old body under the sheets. Tonight, he watched her lay her head on the pillow, hair cascading down her back, hoping it wasn't the last time he'd witness Mary's nighttime routine. As he scooted in behind her, he rested his cheek on her soft red curls and felt her uneven breathing as he wrapped his arms around her.

"Goodnight, sweetie," he whispered as he kissed her cheek. "I love you."

Mary rolled over to face Jack. "I love you, too, dear. I'll be glad when this trial is over so we can go back home."

"I'm glad you're so confident. You could be going home without me, you know." Jack's lip quivered as he said the words, but his eyes remained dry. No, he wouldn't cry, he thought. He had to stay strong for Mary.

"I won't even think about that possibility. You have no criminal record, you're the kindest man I know and, best of all, there were no witnesses to your altercation. There's no way they can convict you."

Jack smiled. "Leave it to you to find the silver lining. No witnesses could make it pretty difficult to throw the book at me." He chuckled, but he wondered if there had been a witness. Did he trip on some inanimate object when he planted his face on the deck or did someone grab his foot as he was rushing toward Vern. Had the concussion caused him to confuse the events of that day? He could have sworn it was a hand that pulled him down, not an accidental fall. Just because he was sixty-nine years old, didn't mean he was one of those old codgers who would trip over his own feet—old and fragile wasn't in his vocabulary.

"You're a million miles away, Jack. What were you thinking?"

"Oh, nothing. Just wondering if young Will Fuller is up to the task of defending me. He's not much older than my grandson, for God's sake." Jack laughed. He didn't want to worry Mary with his thoughts of a possible witness. He'd keep that concern to himself.

"Will has been wonderful so far. He may be a kid, but at our age everyone is a kid. I'm pretty sure I heard him say he was over thirty." She giggled as she touched Jack's face. "I believe he has what it takes to win this case."

"Look at us, Mary. We're on the eve of a trial that may separate us forever and we're laughing."

"I want to keep smiling and laughing with you right up to the last moment we're together. That's the thing I love about you, Jack Madison. You had me giggling on our first date and I haven't stopped since."

"I promise you we'll get through this, and I hope to God we have at least twenty more years of love and laughter—uninterrupted!"

****

Lying next to each other, staring at the ceiling, Justin and Annie overheard their grandparents laughing through the wall. Their San Francisco condo with its stunning panoramic view of the city and the bay brought joy to Justin's heart every time he thought about the journey he and Annie had taken to get here. While perfect for the two of them, sharing the space with Jack and Mary had put a strain on all four of them. Between the paper-thin walls separating their bedrooms and the competition for the TV remote, Justin felt like a guest in his own home. Not that he minded Mary and Jack preparing meals for him and Annie after a long day in the tech jungle, but honestly it would be nice to have the place to themselves again.

"I'm so looking forward to the day we can make love out loud again," Justin whispered.

Annie giggled, "I know, babe. It will be nice to chase you around the living room naked."

"You didn't do that before, but I'm game." Justin rolled over and draped his arm around her lean, olive-skinned body. "I shouldn't be laughing. We need to focus on the trial. I know my grandpa is innocent, but I'm still worried the jury won't see it that way."

Annie returned Justin's embrace. "We need to laugh to relieve the tension. It's not going to change the outcome and God knows we can't fool around—at least not like we'd like—with them in the next room."

"Yeah, it feels good to laugh." Justin said. "I'm glad we've been able to have some good times with Grandpa Jack and Mary these last two months. I think they enjoyed exploring our city."

Annie smiled. "I enjoyed touring the city myself. I'm still a newbie after only a couple of years here. You've been in the bay area your whole life. Seeing it through your eyes has been wonderful for them and for me."

"Well, I think they've seen it all now, so it's time to get this trial over with and send them back to Seattle. I have a good feeling about their attorney. I think Grandpa's in good hands, and we'll be sending our house guests home very soon."

"Hope so. I'll be so glad to get this over with, but now I need to sleep. Good night, Justie. Love you."

"Love you, too, babe." Justin pulled her close and wrapped his arm more tightly around her. He closed his eyes, but sleep did not come easily.

****

Darlene was stuck. She wanted out of this mess, but she knew Robert would never let her go; she knew too much. Where would she go anyway? Her mother made it clear there was no room for her in Puerto Vallarta. Was Vern living with her? Was he actually alive? Not that she really wanted to live with her mother, but she desperately wanted to escape. As much as she wanted to run away, she knew she could not make a move now. Robert's anger had been bubbling closer to the surface as it was. What would he do to her if she sabotaged his credibility just as the trial was about to start? So, moving in with her mother or friends wasn't an option.

Friends, what a joke. She'd alienated any friends she might have had when she hitched her wagon to Robert's star. Who needed them anyway when she had great sex and a handsome man by her side, a man who spared no expense when it came to buying her gifts? What more did she want? The truth was, she wanted a lot more than she was getting with a schemer like Robert. She couldn't believe she was even thinking those thoughts—Darlene Dunwoody, master schemer was finally seeing how unattractive her actions had been. Watching Robert lie and manipulate was like looking in a mirror and she didn't like the reflection. The last two months, waiting for Jack's trial, brought her conscience to the forefront and now she knew that no amount of money was worth sacrificing a man's life. But for the moment, she would play the game with Robert.

The two of them sat on opposite ends of the couch, more common these days as they drifted farther apart. Darlene read her book, a romance novel transporting her to a world where the hero showered his woman with love and respect, something sadly lacking in her current situation.

"Bobby, are you ready for bed?" Tomorrow he might be an asshole, but tonight she'd take advantage of his sexual favors. Maybe it would relieve some of the tension.

"I will be in a few minutes. I'm going over my testimony—it's got to match the deposition they took last month." Robert said as he went over a pile of notes he'd been scribbling.

"If you just tell the truth you won't have to worry about keeping your story straight." Darlene's voice, normally soft and sensual, held an edge that reflected her disapproval. "What exactly are you planning to say, or should I ask?"

Robert's eyes bored into hers, reminding her of the fear she'd felt recently. "As I've told you over and over, I plan to tell the truth as I see it," he said, spewing the words through tight lips.

"I know how you see it, Robert, and you can't go through with your eyewitness account. I know we could use the money, but I'm having second thoughts. I can't let you send an innocent man to prison. It's just not right."

"Since when have you worried about doing what's right? You and I are two of a kind. We take what we can get any way we can get it."

"Not anymore. I can't do this."

Robert shoved the pile of notes off his lap and shot toward Darlene's side of the couch. His blue eyes flashed like the tip of a hot flame. He grabbed Darlene's wrist and brought his face so close to hers she gagged on the smell of whiskey.

His voice was deliberate. "You *will* do this, and you *will* keep your mouth shut if you know what's good for you. If you mess this up, you'll be sorry."

Darlene cowered. "What are you gonna do? Are you going to hit me again? You're no better than your father."

Robert tightened his grip. "Don't ever compare me to my father, ever!"

"You're hurting me, Bobby. Stop! Let go! I promise I won't say anything. Do what you need to do. I won't get in your way."

Robert released her wrist and backed off. "That's my girl." He smiled.

Darlene forced a half smile. "I'm going to bed. Tomorrow's going to be a long day."

Robert looked up from his pile of papers. "I'm right behind you."

"Take your time." Darlene tried to speak as calmly as possible. She didn't want to upset Robert, and she'd definitely lost her desire to use him for her orgasmic pleasure. "If I'm asleep by the time you get to bed, please don't wake me." Leaving her book on the table, a book that painted a very different picture of romance than her lust-based union with Robert, she rose and turned for the bedroom. There was more to life than the superficial crap Robert was dishing out. For now, she was stuck, but she would find a way out—she had to.

Chapter Twenty-Seven

A New Life

Gladys stretched out on the white chaise lounge on the balcony nodding off occasionally as the morning sun warmed her face. In her wakeful moments, she contemplated her situation with Vern. She'd been "the other woman" for over thirty years, succumbing to Vern's whims and wishes in exchange for a few—make that quite a few—extra dollars thrown her way. Life had been more comfortable for her and Darlene with the extra "overtime" pay and along with the funds she'd skimmed off the books, Gladys could live out her golden years in financial security. The fact that she'd had to sleep with Vern to reach her goal hadn't bothered her at the time, in fact, there had been a time when she felt she was truly in love with the guy. But that all changed when Mary divorced him. No longer "the other woman", Gladys inherited the dubious role of main squeeze and learned what Mary had known for so long, that being Vern's number one lady changed everything. Suddenly, he acted like she was his property rather than his carefree dalliance and Gladys was not about to be owned. Twice a week on the side was fine but having Vern underfoot every God damn day was an entirely different dynamic, one she could do without.

Although they'd considered living together after

Mary left, Gladys had resisted, keeping her home and making constant excuses to keep Vern at bay. She'd finally come to the conclusion that he wouldn't be so bad in Puerto Vallarta with a couple million dollars and jumped on board with the scheme when Vern and Robert presented their plan. Now she wasn't so sure.

The last two months had shown her the side of Vern that Mary had lived with, a side that was quick to anger and even quicker with a slap or a punch. The bruises were starting to mount up and since the marks of Vern's dominance were hard to hide in summer apparel, she was stuck in the condo day in and day out. If this was what she had to look forward to, she wanted out. Two million dollars might heal her wounds for a short time, but now she understood the old cliché: Money can't buy happiness, at least not if she had to share her life with Vern. When the trial was over and the money was in her hands, she'd find a way to ditch the old bastard.

For now, she would play the game and try her best to keep her mouth shut. Darlene had texted her this morning that the trial was about to start. It wouldn't be long before the insurance company would be obligated to pay—she would soon be out of her misery.

Even behind closed eyes, she felt a dark shadow block her sun. A dark cloud, indeed—she opened her eyes to see Vern towering over her lounge chair.

Vern held Gladys' phone in his hand. "You left your phone in the kitchen, darlin'. I took the liberty of answering it." He offered the device to her. "It's your daughter. She wants to speak to you."

Gladys reached for the phone. "You shouldn't have answered. Now she knows you're alive."

Pulling back the phone with one hand, he grabbed

Gladys' wrist with the other and jerked her to her feet in one swift movement. "She knows all right, and she knows she damn well better keep her yap shut if she knows what's good for her." The fire in his eyes invoked a fear Gladys hadn't previously felt with Vern. Had he changed or was she finally seeing him for who he really was? She struggled to free her wrist. His lips curled in a half-smile as he released her and handed her the phone. Without blinking he held her hostage with his steely gaze. "Now, it's up to you to make sure she understands what might happen to her or to you if she screws this up."

With shaking hands, she took the phone. "Hi, honey. How's the trial going?"

"Oh my God, Mom. Vern's alive? Why didn't you tell me?"

Gladys looked at Vern who was obviously scrutinizing her end of the conversation. "Oh, Darlene, we didn't want to make you or Robert lie. If you didn't know Vern was alive, it would have been so much easier. But now I guess you'll have to keep this information to yourself. We've come this far, so we don't want to sacrifice that payday."

"What if I tell the truth, Mom. I'm not sure the money is worth this?"

"If you have any intention of revealing this, both you and I are going to pay with more than money. I can't stress that enough. I know you'll do the right thing—for all of us." She glanced at Vern and his smile told her she'd passed the test. Her words confirmed the threat Vern had already issued and, hopefully, Darlene would follow his orders.

"I can't promise anything. Vern's an asshole, but he wouldn't hurt you." Darlene said.

"Yes, he would. He and Robert would do anything to save their business. This is the best thing for all of us."

"I gather Vern is listening to you?"

"Yes, he's right here, honey. My other half is finally here with me." She smiled her biggest smile, hoping Vern would not see her utter disdain for the man. In that moment, she made a decision. No more abuse.

"I have to get back to the courtroom, Mom. I hope I won't have to testify."

"That would be nice. Goodbye, honey."

"Bye, Mom. I love you." The phone went dead. Gladys had ended the call.

Vern took the phone from Gladys. "I'll take charge of this. I don't see any reason you need to call anyone."

She was about to protest, but would her words bring another slap? She swallowed hard. "Of course, Vern, there's no one I need to call."

****

The past two months had taken Carmen down a twisted road she never expected to travel—and sadly, the journey was not over. From housekeeper on *The Queen of the Seas* to Vern Bradley's savior, she had traveled the high road. That road took a downward turn when she was seduced by the promise of the kind of cash she would never see in her day jobs, turning her into a kidnapper, and even worse, a blackmailer. Apparently, blackmail required a special skill level she obviously didn't possess. She'd asked for $200,000, reduced her request to $50,000 now, and had received a bank transfer for $5,000—had Robert forgotten the other zero? Not likely. From her few conversations with Robert, she figured his motive was to give her just enough to keep her mouth shut. Carmen pondered her situation, after all, she could serve time for kidnapping if she revealed the truth, but was $5,000 enough to buy her silence? Not even close.

The money did, however, allow her to put Javier in rehab, sober him up, get him off the couch, and secure him a job on *The Queen of the Seas*. With a heartfelt apology for her abrupt resignation and a good word from Harold Stein, Javier was now a member of the kitchen staff and had worked his way up from dishwasher to busboy and he'd even told his mom he had aspirations of moving up the ladder—perhaps he'd be a waiter soon.

Although life was generally too quiet with the apartment all to herself, today was Monday and Harold would be here soon. Javier rarely visited his mother anymore, knowing she found more pleasure with Harold—he understood—he was just as happy to stay onboard with the crew, his newfound home away from home.

The knock on the door brought that familiar rush to Carmen's body. She smiled as she checked her reflection in the hallway mirror on the way to greet her man. The flush of her cheeks contrasted with her raven black hair projected an image she hadn't seen in years. Despite closing in on age fifty, she felt like a schoolgirl again. In the dimly lit hallway, she even looked the part. The knock came again, louder this time. Smoothing the folds of her white cotton sundress, she took the last few steps and opened the door. One look at Harold sent a tingling sensation through her body. How had she passed him by for so many years? Now all she wanted to do was make up for lost time.

Harold's eyes shot sparks her direction. "Wow, Carmen, you look amazing. That white dress is giving me ideas…"

"Harold!" Carmen's cheeks felt hot. "What are you suggesting?"

"It's probably too soon to suggest anything. Let's just say you look beautiful in white." He took her hand and planted a light kiss on her fresh, red lipstick.

Carmen led Harold to the couch. "I know you don't have a lot of time to waste, but I really need to talk to you."

"You're not breaking up with me, are you?" Harold's smile faded.

"Of course not. I promise I still want your body, but I need your mind today."

"You've got my full attention. As much as I want to kiss you, I want so much more from you. What do you need?"

"Well, I've been texting Robert and it seems the trial against Jack Madison started this morning." She took a deep breath. "If Jack is found guilty, the life insurance will pay, and Robert will wire me $200,000. As much as I want that money, I don't want it at the expense of an innocent man."

"What are you saying?

"I'm saying, Robert doesn't have the money to pay me until the trial is over, but think about it, once the trial is over, he has no motivation to pay for my silence. And from what I know of Robert, he wouldn't want to part with any of his precious money."

"So, what are you going to do?"

"As much as I'd like that payday, I'm going to find a way to tell the truth without getting myself in trouble for locking Vern up here." Carmen looked into Harold's eyes, hoping for a sign of approval. "I hope saving his life will make up for holding him hostage."

"It's not your fault. That bastard talked you into keeping his secret in exchange for cash. He was quite convincing, I'm sure." Harold held her hands and his eyes told her he was on her side.

"So, you'd still want me if I had no money?" she said with a half-smile.

"I'm with you, but how are you going to prove he's still alive?"

"We can thank my son for that. Vern took Javier's phone when he left and with the 'find my phone' app, I have an exact location of the phone."

"Carmen, I don't want you for your money and I'm very proud of you for wanting to tell the truth. We could both get into trouble for our role in this, but I think you're right. We need to tell the truth. But let's give it a few days and see where the trial is headed before we put ourselves in the line of fire."

"I agree. I'll check in with Vern's other son, Sam, in a couple of days to see where things stand. Hopefully, he won't hang up on me."

"He won't when you tell him Vern is alive. You don't need that money anyway. Doesn't school start in a couple of weeks?

Carmen smiled. "About that. A teacher's salary doesn't pay much more than head housekeeper on a cruise ship. I talked to HR on *The Queen of the Seas*. They're willing to give me my job back, so I think I'll make that my full-time occupation. Would you get tired of seeing me every day?"

"Not a chance." Harold took her face in his hands and kissed her. "Not a chance."

Chapter Twenty-Eight

The Trial Begins

"…and we, the prosecution, will prove beyond a shadow of a doubt that Jack Madison is guilty of the cold-blooded murder of Vern Bradley." Dick Diamond pointed an accusing finger at Jack as he continued with his opening statement.

Mary sat in the front row, wrapping her fingers in a grip so tight her new wedding ring cut into her fingers—and still she couldn't stop her hands from shaking. Each pounding beat of her heart reminded her there were far fewer heartbeats ahead of her than behind her. With her eyes fixed on the back of Jack's balding head, she wondered if they would share their last chapter together or if he would be taken from her.

Moving her focus to the jury, she perused each face, hoping they weren't buying the prosecuting attorney's distorted view of Jack's story. She shivered when she realized these twelve ordinary people held Jack's life in their hands. Dick Diamond, the prosecuting attorney, was smooth as silk in his pinstriped suit and slicked back hair as he dramatized the events of the alleged murder of Vern Bradley. Where had he gotten those "facts," Mary wondered? With each word he spoke, Mary felt the curtain dropping on Jack's life. Did Diamond know something she didn't know? Had Jack really done it? His concussion had left him without a memory of that fateful day. And now Dick Diamond was doing his best to convince the jury he was the only one in possession of the truth? Judging from their wide-eyed expressions, most of them were buying the bogus picture painted by San Francisco's star prosecutor. Did Jack stand a chance with this guy in charge? According to records, in the past ten years, Diamond had not lost a case.

And now it was Will Fuller's turn to convince the jury to dismiss Dick Diamond's version of the events. His record was not so rosy. Jack's case was his first.

Will scooted his wooden chair back with a scraping sound that brought attention to his awkward rise from his seat. He hesitated a moment, glanced at his notes in a hand that Mary swore was shaking, took an audible breath, and began.

"I ask you, men and women of the jury, to take a good look at the defendant, Jack Madison. He is five feet nine inches tall and weighs no more than one hundred seventy pounds. He is sixty-nine years old and although he's in excellent health, how likely is it that this man could push a man as large as Vern Bradley over the railing of a cruise ship? For the record, Mr. Bradley is six feet two inches and weighs more than he should at approximately two hundred fifty pounds. You'll notice I said "is" rather than "was" as we have no reason to believe he is dead other than hearsay and circumstances. Admittedly, he is missing, but dead? I think not. Something's wrong with this picture and I intend to unravel the mystery one witness at a time. I invite you, the jury, to take this journey with me as we uncover the truth—the truth that will prove Jack Madison is an innocent man."

Mary looked at young Will Fuller with fresh eyes. Although his charcoal gray suit was less imposing than Dick Diamond's pinstripes, he had a young hip style that demanded attention. The tremor in his voice she detected in his first words was long gone by the time he concluded his remarks. She only hoped he could deliver on his promise to uncover the truth.

****

Darlene sat across the aisle from Mary, Robert on her right side, Dick Diamond straight ahead. Why had Robert chosen to sit so close to his mother when they were so clearly estranged? They hadn't spoken since the cruise ended two months ago and now Mary's tear-filled eyes looked straight through Darlene in an obvious effort to capture Robert's attention. He stared straight ahead. Darlene glanced Mary's way then dropped her eyes to her hands resting in her lap. How could she look at the woman who would soon be without her husband if Robert had his way? But she had to go along with the plan, didn't she? If she told the truth, there's no telling what Robert would do to her. And if Robert's fury didn't cause her enough pain, Vern would certainly take over and… She didn't want to think about what Vern might do.

Her thoughts were interrupted by the sound of Dick Diamond's voice.

"The Prosecution would like to call our first witness, Robert Bradley." Diamond's eyes moved to Robert, but not without a lecherous glance at Darlene. God, he gave her the creeps.

Robert stood and stepped over Darlene on his way to the witness stand. Watching him walk with jaunty steps to the stand made it clear to her that he couldn't wait to hang Jack out to dry. Would he really go through with his eyewitness testimony? Watching him place his hand on the Bible and swear to tell the truth, she wondered…

Dick Diamond nodded toward the jury, his smile revealing almost too many sparkling white teeth, then he fixed his gaze on Robert.

"Where were you at approximately 7:00 p.m. on June 4th?" Diamond asked.

Robert didn't hesitate as he recounted his whereabouts. "I was coming up the stairs from the reception when I heard my dad and Jack exchanging words."

"These words. Were they friendly?" Dick asked.

"To be honest, my dad…" Robert started to explain.

"You dad being Vern Bradley?" Diamond interjected.

"Yeah, my dad, Vern, was yelling at Jack telling him he'd never be enough for my mom. I was able to reach the deck unnoticed and I hid behind a post."

"And what did you see, Robert?"

"Jack rushed toward my dad who was twice his size and Dad just hauled off and punched him, sending him across the deck on his ass. Jack got up and it looked like he thought he had superhuman strength—he was all riled up and he sped toward Dad and rammed him in his beer gut. Jack's kind of a puny guy, so it didn't seem like the blow had enough force to push him over the edge. It was, however, enough to get my dad off balance. Dad was leaning back, flailing his arms trying to right himself when that little asshole, Jack, who had bounced off Dad's gut, reached out and pulled my dad's feet out from under him." Robert's voice cracked and he squeezed his eyes as though he was trying to muster a tear. His voice had been escalating and Darlene waited for Robert's final dramatic performance. He bowed his head. "I can understand Jack's head butt. I know my dad could be a jerk at times. But when he pulled Dad's feet out from under him, well that's just cold-blooded murder."

Will Fuller stood up. "Objection. Witness is giving opinion."

"Sustained. Just stick to the facts Mr. Bradley."

Dick Diamond continued. "Why didn't you step in to save your father, Robert?"

"By the time I realized what was happening, it was too late. I never thought that little pipsqueak would be a match for a big man like my father. Dad might have been a little drunk and off balance and it all came together, but since you want facts, I'll give you facts. Jack Madison killed my father."

Dick Diamond looked at the judge. "No further questions, Your Honor." Looking at the jury with what looked like a satisfied smile, he announced. "The prosecution rests."

The crowd let out a collective gasp. One witness and it looked to be a slam dunk with that testimony. Darlene knew she should say something, but the repercussions from both Robert and Vern would likely put her life in jeopardy. How far would they go to keep her quiet?

Chapter Twenty-Nine

In Jack's Defense

Judge Alex Stone rolled her eyes as if she'd seen Richard Diamond's theatrics before. "Are you sure you want to rest your case, Mr. Diamond?"

"Yes, Your Honor. We would, however, like to reserve the right to call future witnesses after the defense presents their case if new evidence comes to light."

Darlene was glad they hadn't called her as a character witness for Robert. In most cases there would be a corroborating witness and if that wasn't possible, someone would be called to attest to the character of the eyewitness. Obviously, Robert told his attorney that no one would vouch for his moral fiber. She certainly wouldn't and it seems he knew she was reluctant to lie for him.

Judge Stone nodded her head. "All right then. Let's move on. Mr. Fuller, do you wish to cross examine Mr. Bradley?"

Will bolted out of his chair. "You bet your…I mean, yes, Your Honor, I would like to cross examine Robert Bradley."

"Your witness, Mr. Fuller. And you don't need to bet your backside on this trial. I realize you're new, but let's keep to the script from now on."

"Yes, Your Honor."

"Much better." Judge Stone smiled and nodded to Will.

Will took a deep breath, fixed his gaze on Robert, and began.

"Mr. Bradley, you and your father, Vern, were business partners. Is that correct?"

"Yes. Technically, my father was the owner. I'm considered an employee."

"As an employee, were you satisfied with your salary?" Will asked

"Yeah, I guess so. I do all right."

"Just all right? Would you have done better as a full partner?"

Dick Diamond stood up. "Objection, Your Honor. Not relevant."

"Sustained. Just stick to the facts of this case. What is your intention with this line of questioning?"

"Your Honor, we believe the discrepancy in income is relevant and I would like to pursue the financial ramifications of Vern Bradley's alleged death."

Judge Stone hesitated, looking over some notes. "I'll allow a little leeway, but only as it pertains to this case. We do not need to know Robert Bradley's personal income. Go ahead."

Will continued "Mr. Bradley, It is my understanding that your salary was actually a drain on the business. You would have made less as a partner as the business was suffering. Is that correct?"

Robert's voice was steady. "We've had a few tough months, but I would not say we were suffering. We always land on our feet."

"So, you weren't in need of any additional cash to make payroll or complete your current construction jobs?"

"We have a line of credit that kept us afloat. We've had those reversals before and as I said, we always get through them." Robert said.

"That's good to know, but it's probably timely that you stand to collect a hefty life insurance settlement once it's determined that your father did, indeed, fall overboard. I am assuming, as in most businesses, there is a large life insurance policy on the owner of Bradley & Sons. Is that the case with your father? Did the firm take out a policy on his life?"

"Yes, that's standard business practice."

"And how much would you stand to gain if your father died?"

"Objection," Diamond yelled.

"Sustained."

"Let me rephrase that," Will said. "What was the death benefit of that policy?"

Robert glared at Will but answered speaking so softly Darlene barely heard his voice. "Five million dollars."

"For those of you in the jury box who couldn't hear that, I'll have the court reporter read that back." He turned to the court reporter. "Would you please read Mr. Bradley's response in a voice loud enough for the courtroom to hear?"

The clicking of computer strokes stopped for a moment as the reporter answered in a strong voice. "Five million dollars."

Will smiled at the jury, nodded to the judge, and fixed his gaze on Robert. "No further questions, Your Honor."

****

Mary watched her firstborn son step down from the witness stand, her gaze never wavering from Robert as he walked toward his seat. He turned his face away from her, obviously avoiding any possible eye contact. As he opened the wooden gate and stepped to the aisle that separated their seats, Mary stood up.

"Look at me, Robert." He continued to his side of the aisle without responding. "I said look at me, God damn it!" The judge's gavel broke through, pounding rhythmically in an obvious effort to stop Mary's rant, but Mary continued through the noise. "I didn't raise you to be a liar and I know with every fiber of my being that your story is one big lie." With the gavel still beating, Mary's voice cracked, and her tone softened. "What happened to you, Robert? What the hell happened to you?"

Judge Stone nearly broke her gavel when she finally spoke. "Order in the court. I'll have no more outbursts on my watch. If you find the need to shout at this witness again, I will hold you in contempt. Now, sit down!"

Mary plopped down on the hard bench with a thud. "I'm sorry, Your Honor." She said the words, but she wasn't a bit sorry she'd told Robert how she felt. Dabbing her eyes with the tissue she'd been holding to catch any stray tears, she used her other hand to massage the bruise that was forming on her backside from her abrupt drop to the bench. Then she heard her name.

Will Fuller was feeling confident now and it came through in his tone. "The defense calls Mary Bradley Madison."

Still rubbing her ass, Mary stood up and walked to the witness stand with her head held high, red curls bouncing with every step. When she reached her destination, she slapped her hand on the Bible, stated her full name, and swore to tell the truth, the whole truth, and nothing but the truth, then she gently set her bruised butt on the chair. She was ready to defend her man.

Will flashed his blue eyes on the jury, then turned to Mary. "Mrs. Madison when we spoke previously, you told me that you were the first person on the scene after your husband and Vern Bradley had their alleged altercation. Is that correct?"

"Well, I thought I was the first one there, but it seems someone else beat me to him. No one was looking after Jack or calling for help, so I would have to say I was the first person there that actually gave a damn. I can't believe Robert, my own flesh and blood, would walk away from someone in pain." Mary looked at Robert as she spoke.

Dick Diamond shouted. "Objection, your Honor."

"Sustained. Just answer the questions, Mrs. Madison. We want facts, not opinions," Judge Stone said looking straight at Mary.

Will continued. "And why were you so concerned, Mrs. Madison?"

"Jack was lying face down on the hard deck, unconscious, for God's sake. I know I should stick to the facts, but the fact is someone should have called for help." Mary voice escalated as she relived the day. "If I hadn't come looking for him God knows how long he would have lain there."

"Do you have any reason to believe your ex-husband Vern Bradley might have hit him? Or were his injuries consistent with a fall?" Will asked.

"I have lots of reasons to believe Vern hit him. Vern hit me for forty years as well as his two sons. I can't believe Robert is defending his father after all he went through."

Dick Diamond jumped up again. "Objection. We are not here to disparage the victim."

Will spoke up before the judge could answer. "Your Honor, I am only trying to set up the reason for this altercation. Previous confrontations that evening and prior behavior by the victim need to be noted to understand the nature of this argument. I believe the jury should be aware of those facts."

Judge Stone answered. "Objection overruled. I'll allow this line of questioning, but Mr. Fuller please don't drag this out. Just give us an overview."

Will paused. Was he going to be able to paint a picture of Vern's true nature? Mary held her breath hoping he would ask her the right questions. Then he cleared his throat and began.

"Mrs. Madison, when did you find out your ex-husband, Vern Bradley, was on your cruise?"

"At my wedding reception. Jack and I had just tied the knot and were about to cut the cake when Vern showed up."

"And was he coming to congratulate you on your nuptials?"

"Oh no, he was there to tell me our divorce wasn't legal, because we're Catholic and all. But I told him I quit that damn church. I tried to stick it out, but no God of mine would agree with the Catholic mantra of lifelong marriages no matter what."

"And why didn't you want to stay in your marriage to Vern Bradley?"

"Because I was tired of being his punching bag and when he showed up at our wedding reception, I told him

I was done with the Catholic church and done with him. He didn't like my answer and kept coming for me, so I tried to slap him, but he grabbed my arm. Luckily, Jack, his grandson, Justin and my other son, Sam, came to my rescue and Vern let go. Seeing he was outnumbered, he left but not before threatening both me and Jack."

"Can you tell me what he said that felt like a threat?" Will asked.

"Vern said I was still his wife because of our Catholic ties, then he said to Jack, 'Stay away from my wife or you'll be sorry.' Jack asked if that was a threat and Vern in his booming voice said, 'No, it's a promise.' That's a phrase I heard many times during my marriage to Vern."

Will looked toward the jury, then back to Mary. "So, were you surprised to find Jack had been assaulted by Vern?"

"Objection." Diamond bellowed.

"Sustained."

Will smiled. "Sorry, Your Honor."

Mary smiled, too, knowing the jury heard the words. The judge may have told them to ignore the assault accusations by sustaining the objection, but those words were locked in their heads now.

"So, what happened after you found Jack?"

"I screamed and my family, except Robert, came running to help. Jack's daughters were right there with me when he regained consciousness—he thought he was looking at three beautiful angels. My other son, Sam, and Jack's grandson stepped in and carried Jack to the ship's doctor."

"And what were the results of his medical evaluation?" Will asked.

"He had a concussion."

"How did that affect his recollection of the altercation?"

"He remembered that Vern confronted him when he was on the deck taking a cigar break. And he remembered Vern shoved him. But all the other details have been lost due to his concussion. He just can't remember exactly how he ended up on the floor."

"Has his memory come back since the incident?"

"Bits and pieces, but nothing substantial."

"Thank you, Mrs. Madison." Will turned to the judge. "No further questions, Your Honor."

Judge Stone nodded to Will then looked toward Dick Diamond. "Do you wish to cross examine the witness Mr. Diamond?"

"Yes, Your Honor." Richard Diamond bolted from his chair to within inches of Mary's face. "I have only one question. Mrs. Madison, we heard the words your ex-husband allegedly used to 'threaten' you and Jack, but you forgot to mention Jack's response. I understand he threatened to kill Vern. I believe his exact words were, 'stay away from my wife or I'll kill you'. Is that true?"

"Well, he didn't mean that literally," Mary said.

"I really don't care what he meant. I want to know if he said those words. Did he or didn't he, Mrs. Madison? Did he say he would kill Vern Bradley?"

Mary's heart skipped a beat. "He didn't mean it."

"Yes, or no? Did he say he'd kill Vern Bradley?"

Mary hesitated, her eyes filling with tears.

Diamond stared into her tear-filled eyes. "Just answer the question. Yes, or no?"

Mary whispered. "Yes."

Dick Diamond flashed his signature smile. "No further questions, Your Honor."

Chapter Thirty

Darlene's Dilemma

Darlene couldn't take her eyes off Mary as she stepped down from the witness stand. In a matter of minutes, the woman who walked with sure steps and her head held high to defend her husband appeared to have lost her resolve. Dick Diamond had a way of shoving the knife into his victims and twisting it until they spit out the words he wanted the jury to hear.

Robert patted Darlene's knee and whispered, "I can feel the money rolling in. Diamond nailed it with that last statement. We got this, babe."

"At what price?" Darlene looked at him with fresh eyes, eyes that had not seen his true character until this moment. Sure, she knew he'd made some slick deals and may have stretched the truth a time or two, but she never thought he was pure evil. Now she wondered.

Judge Stone interrupted their whispers with a strike of her gavel. "We will take a short recess until 2:00 p.m."

Robert grabbed Darlene's hand. "Let's get out of here."

"No, I'm not going with you." She pulled her hand free.

"What do you mean you're not going with me. You better not be thinking of putting a wrench in the works." Robert grabbed her wrist in a vise grip.

"No, I won't spoil your plans. I know I'd pay a high price for fucking with you and your dad. I'll keep my mouth shut, but I'm not going back to the hotel with you." His eyes seemed to shoot sparks as he gripped tighter. "And you better let go of me with all the eyes in this courtroom on you. I won't hesitate to scream if you manhandle me here."

He let go of her wrist. "I'm sorry. Don't mess this up. We're almost there, baby. Don't leave me now."

"We can talk later. I need some time alone." She gave him a half smile. "I'm going for a walk."

"I need you to come with me." Robert's blue eyes cut through her and sent a shiver down her spine.

"No, Robert. I'm staying right here. Please go." She turned away from his icy stare and walked out of the courtroom and across the hall into the Ladies Room. He couldn't follow her there, but would he be waiting for her when she came out?

Darlene wasn't surprised to see Mary in the Ladies Room. She'd watched her walk that direction and when Darlene stepped through the door, she found Mary at the sink washing her hands.

"Mary, do you mind if I ask you a question?" Darlene asked.

Mary looked up but didn't smile. "What could you possibly want from me? Haven't you and Robert done enough to ruin my life, not to mention Jack's life?"

Darlene hung her head, took a deep breath, then lifted her gaze to Mary's green eyes. The sadness she read in Mary's face convinced her she was making the right decision. "Mary, I wouldn't blame you if you told me to go to Hell, but before you do, I want you to know I can help you and Jack. I know Vern is not dead."

"Why should I believe you? Why haven't you come forward with this sooner?" Mary's voice was shrill.

"To be honest, I'm afraid of Robert and Vern. They would do anything to prevent me from telling the truth. But I can't continue this charade. I want to tell your lawyer what I know. Can you give me his number?" Darlene watched Mary's eyes grow wide and her lips curve into a smile that seemed to stretch her face to its limits.

"Oh my God. Please tell me you're not toying with me. Where is Vern?" Mary asked.

"That's the problem. I don't have a specific address, but I know he's living in a condo in Puerto Vallarta with my mother, Gladys."

"Gladys Dunwoody? Vern's office assistant? Why would he be with Gladys?"

"You didn't know they were together? I thought that's why you left Vern. He's been sleeping with my mother most of my life—over thirty-five years."

Mary gasped, then laughed. "I left him because he beat the crap out of me. The old goat had a lot of energy to jump on me nearly every night and now you're telling me he still had energy for your mother. I'm glad to know he's alive for my husband's sake, but if Jack wasn't accused of his murder, I wouldn't have shed a tear if that bastard had fallen overboard."

"I'm beginning to understand." Darlene surveyed Mary with fresh eyes. This woman was tough, but kind, and Darlene knew what she had to do. "So will you give me Mr. Fuller's number?"

"You bet I'll give it to you if it will help my husband. Thank you, Darlene." Mary's eyes filled with tears and her voice was a mere whisper. "Sometimes our saviors don't look like we expect."

Knowing she didn't deserve such praise, Darlene quietly took down the contact information for William Fuller. If she wasn't able to catch him during this recess, she'd call him tonight right after she moved herself out of Robert's room. One more minute with Robert was a minute too long.

****

Sam didn't recognize the number coming through on his cell phone, but the fact that the number originated from Mexico was a red flag. It had to be the crazy lady who thought he was Robert. What could she possibly want with him? He considered not answering, but curiosity got the better of him.

Sam tapped the screen to answer the call. "Hello?" There was only silence on the other end. "Did you get the wrong son again?"

Carmen finally answered. "No, you are the son I wanted to contact. I want to give you some information on your father."

"Who are you? What do you know about my father?" Sam asked.

"My name is Carmen, and I am a housekeeper on *The Queen of the Seas*. I found your father unconscious on June 5th, the day after he supposedly fell overboard. I nursed him back to health and snuck him off the ship. He convinced me to keep quiet so he could collect some insurance money and I fell into the trap. At the time, I had no idea someone would be tried for murder to collect the money."

"How do you know someone is being tried for murder?" Sam asked.

"Robert let it slip when he was trying to avoid

paying me the reward Vern promised for saving his life. He said he couldn't pay me until there was proof of death and that a confession from his ex-wife's new husband would do the trick. The insurance would pay and then he would pay me."

"And you were okay with that?" Sam asked.

"At first, I thought it was a case of man falling overboard—not murder, so it seemed harmless. Vern told me they had paid through the nose for the policy and the insurance company could afford it. I bought into it, not knowing just how large the policy was. But when I found out a few days ago that there would be a murder trial, my conscience got the better of me."

"So do you know where my father is?"

"I have an exact location. He stole my son's phone and we have located it with the 'Find My Phone' app. I am willing to testify if I can have immunity for holding Vern against his will for a few days."

"I can't promise you immunity, but if this story is true, our attorney will do his best to grant your request. I'll give you his phone number and if he wants you to testify, I'll wire the money for a plane ticket. How soon can you get here? Is there a red eye from Puerto Vallarta to San Francisco?"

"I will check but no promises unless your lawyer can assure me I'll get no jail time."

"Why don't you call him. His name is William Fuller. He can tell you if you're safe. If so, have him call me with your contact information and I'll send you the money for a plane ticket. I'll text you his number."

"Thank you. I promise I will help you find your father."

"I am the one who should be thanking you. You

have no idea what it means to us to have proof of Jack's innocence. Please give Mr. Fuller a call right away. The trial will resume in an hour. I hope to see you tomorrow—and thank you again." Sam ended the call, knowing his wife had been hovering over his shoulder for most of the conversation.

"Well?" Jamie asked as if she was expecting details.

Sam didn't hesitate. He grabbed Jamie, hugged her tight, and spoke through his tears. "Your dad is innocent. We have proof."

Clinging to Sam as tears filled her eyes, Jamie said the words she now knew were true. "My dad is innocent."

****

Will Fuller sat at the defendant's table contemplating his course of action. As a stray lock of his chestnut brown hair fell across his forehead, he reached up to slick it back. He needed to look professional in his first trial. After the recess his next witness would be Jack. He could easily show the jury what a sweet, harmless old man Jack Madison was, and it shouldn't be hard to convince them that Jack didn't have the strength or stature to push a big man like Vern overboard. Will was confident in his approach, but he couldn't help worrying about Richard Diamond's cross examination. The "Dick" as most defense attorneys referred to him, was known to turn cases around with his shrewd and manipulative tactics. Will would not let that happen.

"Excuse me, Mr. Fuller." Darlene said as she tapped him on the shoulder.

Will jumped out of his chair with a start and found himself within inches of Darlene's violet-blue eyes. "I'm sorry, I didn't hear you come in."

"You did look deep in thought," Darlene said.

"I was, but I can take a minute. What can I do for you? I was under the impression you were on the other side of the aisle. Are you here to sabotage my defense?"

"Just the opposite, Mr. Fuller. I think I can help you win your case, but you need to protect me."

"From whom?" Will asked

"From Robert Bradley and his father, Vern, the alleged deceased."

"Alleged? Do you know something I don't know?"

"You bet I do. Vern Bradley is alive."

Giving in to the relief he felt, Will reached out to Darlene and wrapped her in a tight hug. Then pulled back. "I'm so sorry. That was totally inappropriate."

"It's okay. But we need to talk about how we can get this information out without putting me in danger. Can we meet later?"

"I'll meet you across the street at the coffee shop at 4:00. Will that work for you?"

"I hope so." She turned to leave and there he was—staring at her with those ice blue eyes. How long had Robert been watching?

Chapter Thirty-One

Like Father, Like Son

Robert sauntered over to Darlene and looked Will Fuller in the eye. "You trying to steal my girl?" Despite Robert's obvious effort to remain calm, Darlene could tell he was about to explode. She knew him well enough to know he would keep cool in front of the defense attorney, saving his wrath for her later.

"Mr. Bradley, it's nice to finally meet you. I have no intention of stealing your girl but was considering calling her as a witness. Would she corroborate your testimony?"

"Of course she would, wouldn't you, honey?" With his fingers digging into Darlene's side as he wrapped his arm around her, she knew how she was supposed to answer that question.

"Yes, Robert. I believe you. Of course, I believe you." Darlene said using the perkiest tone she could muster.

Will caught Darlene's eye, then quickly averted his eyes to Robert. "Well, in that case," Will said, "I will call Darlene to testify tomorrow. Today we will hear Jack's account of the altercation."

"Fine," Robert said. "Darlene, we need to go now."

"I'll be right there," Darlene said.

"No, you need to come with me now." Robert

grabbed Darlene's hand and pulled her away from Will.

Glancing over her shoulder, she hoped Will would see the fear in her eyes. She needed him to do whatever was necessary to help her get away from Robert.

Reaching the outside corridor, Darlene's voice returned. "Don't you ever talk to me like that again. I've had enough of your controlling bullshit. I'll play your game through this trial, then I'm out the door. I don't want to work for you or sleep with you or have anything to do with your dirty money. I'm done."

"You can't mean that, babe. We're in this together and soon we'll be sitting pretty and able to just relax with our money. It'll be good again when this is over. I promise."

"You're always making promises you don't keep. Now let go of my hand and let me be."

"I'll never let you be. You're mine and I intend to keep it that way." Robert squeezed her hand tighter.

"I don't belong to you or anyone else. You let go of me or I swear I'll scream. I'm not your property, Robert Bradley. Now let me go!" Darlene pulled her hand free and marched to the elevator. She had a lot to do before 2:00 p.m. when the trial would resume.

****

Gladys thought Vern would never leave the house, but when the whiskey ran dry, he was out the door heading for the nearest liquor store. She figured it would take about an hour for him to make the trip, so she had time to do what she needed to do. That bastard would pay for the abuse he'd been dishing out. Unlike Mary, Gladys wouldn't put up with that shit—Mary took it for forty years, but Gladys was done after forty days. She'd spent the last three weeks coming up with a solution to her problem and now she knew how to quell the beast. He wouldn't be causing anyone any trouble after she carried out her plan.

After she used the screwdriver to loosen the bolts on the balcony railing, she wiped her fingerprints off the handle and left it out on the counter. She'd ask Vern to screw or unscrew something—she'd think of a project. That way, when the cops came it would look like he loosened the bolts and was planning to push Gladys off the balcony. Vern had a habit of leaning on that railing, watching Gladys soak up the Mexican sun in her white bikini. She could cover the bruises with spray tan to look her best in tomorrow's sunlight—even at sixty her body was still beautiful, and she knew it. Life would be good again with that asshole out of her life. What could go wrong?

****

Once the elevator reached the lobby, Darlene headed out to catch a taxi to the hotel. It was only a few long blocks away, but she had to hurry. When she got to the hotel, she had the cabbie wait while she rushed to her room and threw her clothes and any loose items into her bag. What would Robert do when he found her gone? At this point she didn't care—she just wanted to get the hell out of his sites. He'd finally gone too far, framing an innocent man for murder with his "eyewitness" testimony.

With a quick zip of her bag, she pulled up the handle and rolled it to the door. Before she reached the door, it opened to a very angry Robert Bradley.

"Where do you think you're going, Darlene?" Robert glared at her.

"I'm moving to another hotel."

"I'm not going to let you do that. I can't afford to let you out of my sight right now. I have a feeling you're going to blow this for us."

"So what if I do? Are you really okay with letting Jack hang for a murder that wasn't committed?"

"Doesn't bother me a bit. Why should I care about the guy who took my mother away? She cares more about him than her own sons."

"Just because she loves Jack doesn't mean she doesn't love you and Sam. She's a good woman, Robert, and Jack's a good man. Better than your father."

Robert grabbed her shoulders and shook her. "Don't you ever compare my father to Jack. My father may have slapped me around a little, but he made a man out of me."

"What kind of man, Robert? The kind of man that uses his fist to make a point? I know if I stay with you any longer, you'll start on me. You've already pushed the limit a couple of times. How far will you go next time?" Darlene watched his face grow red with anger and as his hand came flying at her face, she ducked enough to avoid the full force of his anger. She took that moment to back away from his flailing arms. "I'd be careful about striking me in the middle of this trial. How would it look if the jury saw that the star eyewitness was a wife beater?"

"You're not my wife yet."

"And if you keep up your father's legacy of abuse, I will never be your wife. If you don't change your testimony, I'll leave you for good. But for now, I just want to be alone. I can't even look at you." Darlene pushed past him with her bag in tow. He tried to grab her, but she pulled away. "Don't even think about stopping me."

Robert backed off and spoke in an uncharacteristically quiet tone. "Can we talk later, baby?"

"I don't know. Something's got to change if you want to keep me around." Despite saying she couldn't look at him, she turned to see his ashen face, blue eyes wide with what looked like fear. And did she see a tear forming? Was he putting on an act or did he really care? How could she feel both love and hate for this guy? He hadn't always been such a mean-spirited jerk, but in the past few months she felt like he had changed to the point of no return. She couldn't live on the memory of the Bobby she met as a young girl. He wasn't that man anymore—she had to face the truth. Robert Bradley had become no better than his father.

"Goodbye, Robert." She turned down the hallway toward the elevator and didn't look back.

****

Robert felt a tear roll down his cheek. "What the hell's wrong with me? I don't need a lippy bitch like Darlene in my life. I don't cry and I'm not going to cry over her." He said the words, but his brain didn't hear his plea and the tears stung his eyes as he moved toward the bar in his room to make himself a drink. *Once we have the money*, he thought, *she'll come back to me*.

Chapter Thirty-Two

Jack Tells All

Jack placed his left hand on the Bible and swore to tell the truth, so help him God. Was he cheating if he didn't know if he believed in God anymore? What kind of a God would allow his sweet Mary to suffer abuse for forty years, or put him on trial for murder? As he took his place on the witness stand, Jack wondered if he had done something in particular to piss God off or if life was just a series of ups and downs regardless of your belief in some imaginary man upstairs. Since he had no proof one way or another, he said a little prayer—just in case.

Will rose from his chair, making sure to save his remarks until he was right in front of Jack. He'd reminded Jack to turn up his hearing aids but didn't want to take any chances that his words would be missed.

"Mr. Madison, we've heard that you had an altercation with Vern Bradley. Is that correct?"

"Yes, if you could call it that."

"What would you call it?" Will asked.

"I'd call it a fist in my gut from Vern Bradley and my feeble attempt to fight back."

"And exactly how did you fight back? Did you knock him overboard?" Will turned his eyes to the jury then back to Jack.

"I ran at him and rammed my head into his big beer

gut and bounced off him like I was hitting a big beach ball." Jack tried to keep a serious face, but the image made him smile. He put his hand to his mouth and coughed so the jury wouldn't see his joy as he remembered the blow.

"Did you have enough force to knock him over the railing?" Will asked.

"Oh, God, no. But he did lose his balance and was teetering on the edge." Jack said through the fingers still covering his face.

"So did he fall?"

"I have no idea," Jack said, letting his hand fall from his face as he regained his serious expression.

"You couldn't see whether he fell or not?"

"It's kind of hard to see when you're face down on the deck. I was trying to see what was going to happen when my foot caught on something—or someone—and I fell face down on the deck."

Will looked pointedly at the jury. "I could have sworn the previous testimony of Robert Bradley described your actions much differently. I believe he said you pulled Vern Bradley's feet out from under him causing him to fall overboard. So, are you saying that's not true?"

"Absolutely not true. My collision with that beer gut was the extent of my actions that day." Jack took a deep breath then spoke softly. "I was just defending myself."

"For those of you on the jury who did not hear that response, I'll repeat his words. He said, 'I was just defending myself' and if you look at the facts, Jack Madison was, indeed, just defending himself that day." Will turned back to Jack. "So, tell me, Mr. Madison, what do you think you tripped on that night?"

"I don't think I tripped. It felt more like someone actually grabbed my foot and pulled me down. The only person that says he was there that night was Robert. Maybe he tripped me."

Dick Diamond jumped to his feet. "Objection! Opinion."

"Sustained." Judge Stone said as she turned to Jack. "Please stick to the facts, Mr. Madison."

"Yes, Your Honor."

"I'll rephrase the question." Will looked at Jack. "What made you think someone grabbed your foot?"

"The deck was spotless when we left it after the ceremony. I can't think of anything I could have tripped on."

"Thank you, Mr. Madison. No more questions, Your Honor." Will turned and walked back to his seat.

"Do you wish to cross examine, Mr. Diamond?" Judge Sone asked.

"Yes, Your Honor. I have a lot of questions for this witness." Diamond stood and sauntered toward the witness stand, nodding to the jury as he strode to within a foot of Jack's face. Leaning on the witness stand, Diamond's minty breath assaulted Jack's senses with a cold rush.

Jack leaned back. "Whoa, man, can you back off a little?"

"Oh, am I too close for comfort? Kind of like you were when you pulled Vern Bradley's feet out from under him?"

"Objection," Will shouted.

"Sustained. You know better than to put words in the witness' mouth, Mr. Diamond. I seem to have to remind you of that fact at every trial."

"I'm sorry, Your Honor, I was just trying to establish the proximity of the witness to the victim."

"Alleged victim." Judge Stone corrected. "Let's stick to facts. I don't want to have to correct you again."

"Yes, Your Honor." Diamond turned his attention back to Jack, keeping his distance this time. "So, Mr. Madison, you say you fell on the deck after attacking Mr. Bradley. Did you have any health issues related to that fall?"

"Yes, I lost consciousness, I guess. I woke up with my wife and daughters staring at me like I was dead."

"Did they call for medical attention?"

"My son-in-law and grandson carried me to the elevator and took me to the medical facility."

"And I understand the doctor diagnosed you with a concussion, is that correct?"

"Yes. I had a hell of a headache," Jack said.

"You not only had a headache. You had a lapse in memory due to that fall. Is that the case?" Dick Diamond asked, drilling each word into Jack's brain till it hurt all over again.

"It took me a little time to piece together the incident, but it's all come back to me." Jack was getting agitated, and he felt his heart race with Diamond's methodical prodding.

"How can you be sure it all came back to you? Maybe you forgot something. Previous testimony indicates you pulled Vern Bradley's feet out from under him. Now you're saying you just bounced off his gut and fell on your face. How do we know which story is correct?"

"I may have hit my head, but I'd damn sure remember if I pulled someone's feet out from under them." Jack raised his voice in protest to the accusation.

"But you forgot lots of details for a few days. Why would this be different? Either you forgot this minor detail or you're lying."

Jack's voice quivered. "I'm not the one who's lying. Robert can't possibly be telling the truth. I didn't like Vern Bradley, but I don't have it in me to kill another human being, that much I know for sure—concussion or no concussion."

"Well, we know one of you is lying and the fact that you're on trial for murder makes me think you have the most to gain by bypassing the truth."

"Objection," Will said.

"Sustained."

"Mr. Madison, all I'm saying is your memory may be clouded by that concussion, so we really don't know if you are remembering all the facts. Are you sure you remember everything?"

Jack sighed. "I'll be honest. It took me some time to piece things together, and you're right I have a lot to gain by getting this murder charge off of me, but Robert has a lot to gain by lying, too. I want my life, but he's desperate for that five-million-dollar insurance policy. All I can tell you is it is not in my character to lie or cheat and I dare you to call some character witnesses. I'm honest, sometimes brutally so, and I'm not sure you'd get the same character assessment for Robert Bradley."

"Thank you for your dramatic plea, Mr. Madison. I hope the jury will note that you are desperate to save your life, maybe desperate enough to stretch the truth."

"Objection."

Diamond didn't wait for the judge to rule on that statement but interjected. "No further questions, Your

Honor."

Judge Stone replied. "You may step down, Mr. Madison."

Jack felt the familiar ache in his joints as he stood up. Everyone told him sixty-nine was the new fifty, but today he felt his full sixty-nine years as he stretched his legs before taking the two steps to the floor. He'd said his piece, but Dick Diamond had immediately cast doubt on his words. How would the jury see his testimony? As he approached his seat at the defense table, he raised his head and fixed his gaze on Mary. Her smile looked forced—he knew that look well enough to know she was worried. What more could he have said to plead his case?

****

Jack may have been worried, but Will Fuller was not. He had an ace up his sleeve that would blow this case wide open and he couldn't wait to use it.

Judge Sone interrupted Will's thoughts. "You may call your next witness, Mr. Fuller."

"Permission to approach the bench, Your Honor."

"I assume this is information you don't want to share with everyone." Judge Stone gave him a look that made him question whether he was following procedure.

"I'd like to run this by you before I make any announcements." He looked her in the eye hoping he was not overstepping.

"I'll allow it. Both you and Mr. Diamond may come forward."

Will practically tripped over his chair rushing forward to speak to the judge, speaking before Dick Diamond reached the bench. "Judge Stone, it has come to my attention that there are witnesses to Vern Bradley's whereabouts after the altercation with Jack Madison.

One is afraid to testify, but the other is flying in tonight and would be ready to testify tomorrow. I could fill the afternoon with witnesses attesting to Jack's character, but I'd rather not waste anyone's time if the victim is still alive. We would like to delay the proceeding to at least noon tomorrow?"

"Why weren't these witnesses brought out sooner, Mr. Fuller," Judge Stone asked.

"Honestly, I just found out about both of them today. It seems they had concerns about coming forward."

Dick Diamond overheard Will's revelation and growled, "I need to know who these witnesses are."

Judge Stone replied, "Of course, you are entitled to the witness list. Mr. Fuller, can you share the names of your witnesses?"

"I'll share, but I'm hoping we can protect Darlene Dunwoody from your star witness, Mr. Diamond. It is my understanding that Robert Bradley does not want Ms. Dunwoody to testify. Can you advise him of the dangers of threatening my witness?"

Diamond had few words. "Robert is not my client, so I have no control over him. What I'd like to know is why she defected. Are you coercing this witness?"

"Absolutely not. She came to me," Will said.

"That's enough bickering," Judge Stone said. "Just give me the name of the other witness and why this person needs more time to get here."

"The other witness is in Puerto Vallarta and won't be here until tomorrow morning. Her name is Carmen Miranda. She is an employee of the cruise line, *The Queen of the Seas*."

Diamond raised his voice loud enough for the entire courtroom to hear. "Who the hell is Carmen Miranda?

What does she have to do with this case?"

Will spoke calmly. "I guess you'll find out tomorrow. Or you could ask Robert. He knows very well who this is."

Diamond shouted. "Well, I don't want to delay this trial and if there are no other witnesses, we should be done this afternoon. We should not allow Mr. Fuller to grasp at straws. I'm sure the jury has enough information to make their decision today."

Judge Stone answered. "It's not up to you, Mr. Diamond, and if this woman can provide information pertinent to the case, I will grant a continuum until tomorrow at 12:00 noon."

"Thank you, Your Honor." Will breathed a sigh of relief knowing he would likely win his first case. His only worry was what might happen to Darlene Dunwoody once Robert Bradley found out she was testifying for the defense.

Chapter Thirty-Three

Robert's Wrath

Robert kept an eye on Darlene during the afternoon's proceedings. It was clear she didn't want to sit with him, but he didn't dare let her out of his sight so when she sat in the third row, he sat directly behind her hoping the intensity of his presence would force her to acknowledge him. Even when he tapped her shoulder, she did not turn around—she just slapped at his hand like it was a pesky fly. And now the lawyers were talking to the judge. What could be happening?

Judge Stone ended the silence with a quick but loud rap of her gavel. "Court is adjourned until 12:00 noon tomorrow."

As Darlene rose and headed for the hallway, Robert followed, but again, he couldn't follow her into the Ladies Room. He'd wait for her and make it clear that she had better keep her damn mouth shut. How long could she be in there?

"Robert, we need to talk," Dick Diamond said as he rushed toward his star witness. "Come with me where we can have some privacy."

"I need to wait here for Darlene," Robert said.

"No, you don't. I don't want you talking to her or harassing her, especially in this very public place." Diamond grabbed Robert's arm and pulled him toward a small room across the hall designated for attorneys and their clients.

"Can't you just talk to me out here? I can't let Darlene out of my sight." Robert's heartbeat quickened. He didn't want to come this far and walk away with nothing. Losing Darlene was a crushing blow, but with five million dollars he'd have his choice of a hundred younger, maybe even prettier "Darlenes" who wouldn't be so lippy. He'd had it with her.

"No, Robert, we need to go talk privately." Diamond pulled him into the room.

Robert quit resisting and followed him taking a quick backward glance toward the Ladies Room. "Make it quick, Diamond."

"I'm not sure if I can make it quick. I need to know what your relationship is with a woman named Carmen Miranda."

A wave of anger rolled through Robert's body, but he had to tamp it down. Was that woman going to ruin this for all of them? He took a deep breath and turned to Diamond with a smile and said, "I have no idea who this woman could be. Does she say she knows me?"

"She hasn't said anything yet, but the defense wants her to testify. Will she say she knows you?" Diamond asked.

Beads of sweat were forming on Robert's upper lip. "I can't think of how she would know me—oh, wait—maybe she was the maid we met in my dad's room after he was pushed overboard."

"They don't waste any time cleaning a room after they lose a passenger. I won't ask you why you were in his room, but I'm guessing you haven't told me the whole story. Is there anything you want to add—or subtract—from your testimony? It's not too late to cut your losses if you haven't told the whole truth."

Robert bristled. "Of course, I told the whole truth. If this woman says otherwise, she's lying." He turned to leave the room, then delivered an icy stare to Diamond. "And I expect you to use your considerable skills to prove she's lying. I'm out of here."

****

Darlene peeked out of the Ladies Room in time to see Dick Diamond drag Robert into a small room across the hall. At that moment, she rushed to the elevator and got the hell out of there. It would be an hour before she was to meet Will Fuller at the coffee shop around the corner, but she wasted no time finding the place and taking a seat at a booth in the back where she couldn't be seen from the street. The place wasn't busy—Will must have known the area well enough to set their meeting in an establishment that didn't see a lot of traffic. With a shiny new Starbucks around the corner, this dingy little café didn't stand a chance of surviving, but for now it would provide both Darlene and Will the privacy they needed.

After the server delivered her a cup of coffee, she made sure to tell the woman she was waiting for someone and wouldn't be needing anything else for at least ten minutes. The seclusion of the back booth was perfect for her phone call to her mother. No one would hear her conversation in this little hole-in-the wall. She tapped the screen hoping to find her mother alone and free to talk. After two rings, Gladys answered.

"Hi, honey. How's it going?" Gladys asked in a tone that sounded flat and lifeless.

"Not so well, Mom. I just left Robert and he's

227

pissed. I'm afraid he might come after me if I don't confirm his testimony." Darlene's voice cracked. "I just can't do it. I can't send an innocent man to jail for life when I know Vern is still alive."

"It's okay, honey. Go ahead and tell the truth."

"Really? Aren't you worried about getting your share of the money?" Darlene could hardly believe this was her mother speaking. "Are you okay, Mom?"

"Oh, I'm fine, except for a few bruises from that bastard, Vern. Is that why you left Robert? Was he following in his father's footsteps? They really are a couple of angry men and, frankly, I've had enough."

"I always thought Robert was different, but money really brought out his dark side. He really is no better than Vern." Darlene felt a bond with her mom she'd always wanted, but why did it take a couple of abusive men to finally bring these emotions to the surface?

"We could both do better, honey, and once I have Vern out of here, I'm going to find a new man," Gladys said with a little more animation in her voice. "Life's too short to take that crap from anyone. I'm glad you're getting out, too."

"Yeah, it's a strange feeling, but I know it's the right choice. I just hope I can stay out of Robert's way."

"Get a restraining order," Gladys said in a louder tone. "By the way, did you pay the bill for Vern's life insurance this month?"

"It's on automatic deduction and the insurance company won't pay until there is proof of death. I figured it was worth a few extra payments to collect five million dollars."

"That's good. I'm worried Vern might have an accident, so best to keep that going," Gladys said, her voice taking on a lilting quality Darlene hadn't heard in years. "He's always leaning against the railing of our balcony. It's a long way down from the fifth floor."

"What are you saying, Mom?"

"Oh, nothing. I'm just saying you should keep paying the life insurance. You never know when Vern might meet his maker." Gladys' voice was almost giddy.

"In that case, where should I send the check? You never gave me your new address."

"Oh, I'll let you know when the time comes. It sounds like the trial is not going to bring us the desired result. We'll have to wait a bit longer to cash in."

"What exactly are you saying, Mom?" Darlene looked up at that moment and found Will Fuller's eyes on her. How much had he heard? "I gotta go, Mom. We'll talk later."

"Hello, Mr. Fuller. You're early," Darlene said as calmly as she could after the conversation with her mother.

"Did I interrupt something?" Will asked. A lock of his dark hair fell across his forehead, giving him a less rigid look than the persona he exhibited in the courtroom. His hazel eyes captured hers in a very unsettling stare.

Darlene looked away from the intensity of his gaze. "No, no. I was just talking to my mother. I'm still trying to figure out what's going on down there."

"Tell me more." Will's voice was deep and soothing to Darlene's senses.

"Well, as I told you, I know Vern Bradley is alive. He's living with my mother in Puerto Vallarta. She's been with him—on the side—for over thirty years, but now that he's divorced, things have changed. I don't think she's quite as happy with him on a full-time basis."

"But you're sure he's alive, right?" Will continued to keep his eyes on Darlene. Did the guy even blink?

"Oh, I'm sure, but I don't know how much longer he'll stay that way," Darlene said even as she told herself she should not be sharing these details so freely.

"What do you mean?" Will asked, his brow furrowed with the question. God, he was cute. Darlene felt both trust and attraction to this man and she was not going to deny him any details.

"I mean my mom tried to kill Vern once and I'm not sure she's done trying. It would serve him right. He really is a bastard, but I'm not sure murder is the answer."

"I hope it won't come to that. I'd like to take him down, but I prefer to put the subject of my first case in prison, not in the ground." He laughed revealing a dimple on his left cheek. "Sorry, I know this isn't funny. I'm just so keyed up, I need to release some tension."

"I get it." Darlene smiled for the first time. "I could use a tension reliever myself. I just moved out of my room at the hotel with Robert. I hope he didn't see where I moved. It's an older hotel where he would never think to look—I hope."

"Do you need protection? I could file a restraining order."

"If things don't go his way, I will probably need protection, but if perjury is discovered, can the judge lock him up?"

"Not permanently, but it could give you a little time. But that probably won't happen today, so I think we should file that order."

"What happens if I testify, and he ignores the order? I'm not even sure my testimony would help since I wasn't able to get an address from my mom."

"Well, I have good news for you. You probably won't need to take the stand. I have a witness flying in from Puerto Vallarta who has an exact location of your mother's condo. And she can attest to the fact that Vern was alive after the incident on the ship."

"Really? I don't have to testify?" Darlene sank down into the booth and let out an audible sigh. "Robert will have no reason to come after me then."

Will raised an eyebrow. "Are you seriously worried he might hurt you?" His eyes seemed to look right through her.

Damn, those eyes... Darlene tried to disconnect from his gaze, but the pull was powerful. "I am a little afraid of him. It's funny, I've known Robert since I was a kid and never felt this fear until he started planning this scheme to bilk the insurance company out of five million dollars. He's obsessed and he doesn't want me to screw things up."

Will kept his laser focus on Darlene. "Were you involved in this scheme?"

Darlene turned away from Will's inquiring eyes. "Robert is very persuasive. I went along with the scheme—reluctantly, of course. He convinced me it would look like an accident and, to be honest, it's very hard to say 'No' to Robert or Vern. It was actually Vern's idea and if I wanted to keep my job, I needed to go along."

"Did they threaten you?" Will asked.

"Not in so many words. I was in love with Robert, so I let him lead me astray. And Vern, well, you don't want to cross Vern. He really is a bastard. He beat his wife and kids and now Robert is following in his dad's footsteps. You'd think Robert would avoid violence after being subjected to it all his life, but it doesn't work that way, I guess." Darlene's voice trailed off.

"Is that bruise on your cheek from Robert?"

"No, I slipped in the bathroom and hit my chin on the sink," Darlene lied. "At least that's what Robert is telling everyone. I'm sure you can figure out the truth—he hit me."

"And why did he hit you?"

"Because I told him I was going to tell the truth."

"Well, you won't have to if Carmen gets here in time. Robert can't take it out on you if someone else testifies." Will caught Darlene's eyes again. This time she didn't turn away.

"That's a relief, but does Robert know I'm not going to testify? What am I going to do tonight?" Darlene said as she batted her eyelashes and pushed her lip out in a pout.

Will took the bait. "I'll walk you to your hotel to make sure you're safe. Where are you staying?"

"We might have to take the cable car or an Uber. I booked a room at the Mark Hopkins on Nob Hill."

"When you said an older hotel, I didn't expect The Mark." Will laughed. "You don't do anything halfway, do you, Ms. Dunwoody?"

"Never." She smiled.

****

Will felt the heat sitting next to Darlene on the cable car. She smelled of sweet perfume and her body felt soft and warm next to him. When they arrived at the hotel, she thanked him for the escort and asked him up to her room for a drink.

He could think of about a thousand reasons to go

upstairs with this woman. Maybe she was the love of his life, maybe just an erotic interlude, maybe he was kidding himself to think he could have her, but it seemed she was as interested as he was. The thousand reasons lost their thunder when he thought of the one reason he couldn't go—professional integrity.

Chapter Thirty-Four

The End of the Line

Mary took her place on the bench behind Jack where she could watch the man she loved, even if it was only to stare at the back of his hair-challenged head. Would young Will Fuller come up with a miracle to save Jack? Each day she sat alone in the first row, but today she looked up to see Darlene Dunwoody step in front of her and sit down next to her.

"Hi, Mary. I hope you don't mind if I sit on this side with you."

Mary smiled. "Of course not, dear. I know you haven't always been on my side, in the courtroom or in life, but now that Robert has betrayed me—and you, too, it seems—I'm happy to have you next to me."

"Thank you. I'm sorry about your son. I've loved him since I was a young girl, but he's changed. He used to be so sweet," Darlene said as she broke eye contact with Mary. "What happened to him?"

"I'd like to think he inherited some integrity from me, but it seems he takes after his father. Once he started working for Vern, I lost him."

Mary wanted to know more about Darlene. Was she really a good person or was she playing both sides? She'd been with Robert long enough to know he was not always honest. Was she a schemer, too? Mary started to ask Darlene, point blank, whose side she was on, but she was interrupted by the bailiff's announcement.

"All rise for the Honorable Judge Alexis Stone." As Mary and Darlene stood up, Judge Stone marched to her perch and with a rap of her gavel, the day's proceedings were underway.

"Mr. Fuller, please call your first witness."

"The Defense calls Carmen Miranda to the stand."

Mary looked back to see an attractive middle-aged woman move with tentative steps toward the witness stand. What could she possibly say that would save Jack's skin?

****

Will looked over his shoulder to see Darlene and Mary sitting side by side. He nodded to Mary then erupted into full smile mode when he fixed his eyes on Darlene. Was he blushing? He took a deep breath to get his head together. This next witness would turn the case around and win him a victory, not only in the eyes of the law community, but hopefully, in those enchanting eyes of the woman sitting behind him. He could only hope her defection to his side of the aisle was for real and not some sort of ploy. With all his degrees, excellent reasoning skills, not to mention an exceptional IQ, he still didn't understand women. But he did understand this case and he was ready for Carmen Miranda now that she was sworn in and sitting in the witness seat.

"Good morning, Ms. Miranda. Thank you for coming here today." Will took a long look at the jury, then turned back to Carmen. "I asked you here today because I believe you can shed some light on the whereabouts of Vern Bradley. Is that true?"

Carmen's eyes darted around the room before

answering. "Yes, I believe I can give you an exact location for Mr. Vern."

"And how do you know Vern Bradley is at this location?" Will asked.

"He stole my son's phone when he escaped, I mean, left my home. Javier—that's my son—told me how to locate his phone and now I have an exact location. I assume he is still there because the phone has not changed locations."

"Can you tell me why Mr. Bradley was at your home in the first place? Was he a guest? Tell me exactly how you knew him."

"I met him quite by accident when I was making my rounds to all the cabins on *The Queen of the Seas*. I was head housekeeper on the ship and one of my crew members was—um—sick, so I had to turn down the beds and leave chocolates on the pillows of our guests."

"So, you met Mr. Bradley in his room?"

"I wouldn't say we actually met—at least not right away. I knocked on his door. Usually, passengers are at dinner or out for the evening, so we knock and if there is no answer, we enter the room. When I received no answer from Mr. Vern, I walked in to find him lying on the bed, almost unconscious. I shook him and he didn't budge, so I propped him up—which was not so easy— and I started pouring water down his throat and putting cold, wet towels on his face. He coughed and opened his eyes but wanted to go back to sleep. So, I brewed some very strong coffee and after three cups he was still weak, but awake. Then I was able to get him on his feet. He was unsteady, but with my help he was able to shuffle to the shower where I turned the cold water on him. He swore at me, but he was definitely awake. I continued to encourage him to drink water to dilute the poison he had obviously ingested. After all this, we finally met."

"And when was this meeting?" Will asked.

"June 5th, the night he was supposedly pushed overboard," Carmen said.

"Did he tell you what caused him to pass out?"

"Oh, he was more than just passed out. He had a glass of whiskey and an empty pill bottle on his bedside table. There was a note saying he was going to kill himself."

"So, this was a suicide attempt?"

"Well, it looked like it, but when he woke up, he was very surprised to see that note. He said he had no intention of killing himself and although the handwriting looked like his, he was sure it was written by his long-time office manager and lady friend, Gladys Dunwoody. She knew his handwriting better than he knew it himself, he said."

"Was he angry?" Will asked.

"Oh, angry is not a strong enough word. He told me to take that God damn note and plant it in Gladys' baggage, so she'd see it when she got to her condo. He wanted her to know she hadn't succeeded. I think his anger helped him recover from the overdose—that and his big belly. Those sleeping pills might have killed a smaller person."

"So, you saved his life. Was that the end of your association with Vern Bradley?"

"I am sorry to say that it did not end there. I was about to call the ship's doctor when Mr. Bradley stopped me and told me he was in trouble and needed to get off the ship unnoticed. He swore me to secrecy and promised me $50,000 if I kept quiet and helped him sneak off the

Jacquie May Miller

ship."

"And you helped him without questioning his motives?"

"Oh, I had a lot of questions. He said he had a small life insurance policy that would help keep his business afloat for his son, so they cooked up a scheme to fake his accidental fall overboard. He was very convincing when he told me about the evil insurance company raising the rates, making it impossible to keep paying. He said they'd paid about as much as they would be getting back, so he was going to take his share. I assumed he was telling the truth."

"And was he telling the truth?"

"Not even close. I later found out they were trying to frame Jack Madison for his death and would collect five million dollars, not two hundred thousand as he told me. I know I am probably in a lot of trouble for my part in this. I let greed get the better of me, but when I found out a man's life was in jeopardy, I couldn't continue to hide the truth."

"Thank you, Ms. Miranda. No further questions, Your Honor."

Will walked back to his seat by Jack as Dick Diamond sauntered to the witness stand, flashing his signature smile at Carmen. "So, you say you couldn't continue hiding the truth. It seems you have trouble deciphering truth from fiction."

"Objection." Will stated. "Opinion."

"Sustained. Just ask your questions," Judge Stone said in a monotone.

"The question is, where did you come up with your elaborate story. I understand you're an English teacher. Did you major in creative writing? Who paid you to

238

come up with this one?"

"I teach English as a second language. I do not write fictional stories and, sadly, I am not getting paid to tell the truth."

"Then tell me more about how you held Vern Bradley hostage and tried to blackmail his family for your silence."

"I will admit I wanted the money for saving Mr. Vern's life and I pushed his son, Robert, to pay me. Shouldn't I get something for saving that bastard's life?"

"If, indeed, you saved him and he is truly alive, yes, you deserve thanks. But for blackmail and lying under oath, you probably deserve jail time."

Carmen set her jaw and snapped back. "I have told the entire truth under oath. If you check the location of the phone, I am sure you will find him there with his lady friend."

Richard Diamond paused and seemed to be at a loss for words—but only for a moment—then he spoke in a gentle tone no one had ever heard from the man.

"As most everyone here knows, I'd do anything for win, but Ms. Miranda, you've cast doubt in my mind and even I can't in good conscience convict an innocent man. I can't believe I'm saying this, but I hope you're right. Let's let the authorities take over and see if we still have a case."

Robert leapt from his seat. "What the hell are you saying? Do your job, Diamond."

"Order in the court." Judge Stone shouted with a rap of her gavel.

Diamond responded despite the judge's words, "Mr. Bradley, you seem to forget I'm not your personal attorney. My job is to tell the truth, something I'm learning you know very little about."

Robert responded. "I'm the one telling the truth. That bitch is lying!"

Judge Stone pounded her gavel again. "Enough, Mr. Bradley. Sit down or I'll hold you in contempt and have you thrown out.

Richard Diamond glanced over his shoulder at Jack who was smiling for the first time since the trial began. Will caught the look and wondered if Diamond might be developing a heart. He had to see the broken man Jack had become under the strain of the last two months. Jack may have been smiling, but his furrowed brow told the tale. Even the good news couldn't erase the weight he had obviously been carrying.

"Your Honor," Diamond said, "I can't continue to prosecute Mr. Madison until we investigate Ms. Miranda's claim. I move we recess until we have confirmation of Vern Bradley's status."

Judge Stone's jaw dropped as she focused on Diamond. "Are you serious? I never thought I'd hear a compassionate word from you, Mr. Diamond."

"I admit I go for the throat when I prosecute a case, but even I can't go for this man's throat without checking out this witness' claim."

Judge Stone looked at Will. "If you're in agreement we will wait while your team checks out this location. If Vern Bradley is, indeed, alive, your client will have all charges removed from his record. We'll reconvene tomorrow at 2:00 p.m. Will that give you enough time to verify this claim?"

"Yes, Your Honor, that should be plenty of time." Will smiled and turned to Jack, patting him on the back. "Let's get out of here and go check out the whereabouts of your alleged victim, Jack."

Will made the call to the Puerto Vallarta Police Department and found out there was already a team headed to that exact location. Will asked if they could check out all the condos on the fifth floor while they were there—he'd send pictures of both Gladys and Vern for verification. The officer said he'd pass the information on to his officers but could not promise a quick response as the incident they were investigating might take priority. It might have to wait until tomorrow morning.

****

One hour earlier, Gladys made final preparations for her plan. She had apologized to Vern for God knows what last night and let him have his way with her. Let the bastard think she was back in the fold, she thought. Had he always been this controlling? Probably, but his actions were less noticeable when she wasn't living with him 24/7. Now that she was his main squeeze, she finally knew the pain Mary must have felt. Soon there would be no more pain for anyone.

Gladys knew she looked hot in her white bikini. She may have been sixty years old, but she had a body that belied her years. And with the tan she'd acquired in the Mexican sun, she was ready to give Vern exactly what he deserved.

"Vern, honey, why don't you come sit with me on the balcony."

"I'll be out after I finish tightening the screws on the light switch. I still can't figure how they got so loose," Vern complained.

"Thanks for doing that little chore. Grab a cold beer and come keep me company for a while. I think you'll like what you see." Gladys used a throaty tone that always aroused Vern.

In a matter of minutes Vern appeared, beer in hand and eyes on his woman. "You're damn right; I do like what I see. You look as pretty as you did the day I met you over thirty years ago."

"You're looking mighty fine yourself, Vern." She picked up her phone, stood up, and tapped the screen. "Let me take a picture of you in your favorite spot. Just lean against the railing like you always do and I'll take your picture. I always want it with me."

"Why so sentimental today, darlin'?" Vern asked.

"I just realized we have a pretty good thing here and I want to start enjoying this beautiful place. Look around—the palm trees, the ocean all right in front of us."

"You're right, darlin', but let's both get in this picture. I'll take a selfie of us with the ocean view in the background."

"No, Vern, I don't have any makeup on. Let me just get you for now. You can take my picture later." Gladys said as calmly as she could.

"You look great, Glad. Come here and stand with me." He grabbed the phone and pulled Gladys toward him as he leaned back. The railing cracked under Vern's weight and gave way. His last words were, "You bitch!" as he travelled the five stories to the ground, still holding tight to the hand of his murderer.

The shrill sound of Gladys' scream was the last thing either of them ever heard.

Chapter Thirty-Five

Where There's a Will, There's a Way

Two hours after his call to the Puerto Vallarta Police Department, Will Fuller received the answer he needed, but not the answer he expected. He needed to get to Darlene before the Puerto Vallarta police called her. How would she react to the news? This wasn't the type of information to send in a text, so he decided to call. After several rings, her voicemail intercepted. Why wouldn't she pick up? Hoping she wouldn't hear the news from an outside source, he sent a quick text, telling her to wait for him before answering any calls from her mother's phone or anyone in Puerto Vallarta. Rushing out the door of his courthouse office space, he walked a few blocks to California Avenue and jumped on the cable car that would take him up the hill to The Mark. She'd given him her room number the day before—he was still kicking himself for rejecting her offer to come up for a drink—and now he wasted no time making his way to the elevator that would take him to the tenth floor. Pushing the button, he paced back and forth, waiting...

****

Thirty minutes earlier

Darlene clutched the phone, her heart beating out of her chest as she listened to the man she had once loved. "No, Robert, I will not cover your lies with more lies.

They're going to find your dad alive and there's no way you can talk your way out of this one."

"That's why I need you, baby. I need you to tell them I was trying to protect your mother. She tried to kill him with his own sleeping pills, for God's sake. I was just trying to shift the blame so she wouldn't go to prison."

"But you shifted it to an innocent man. Honestly, my mom is no prize. Maybe she should go to prison." Darlene decided to withhold her mom's most recent confession not knowing if her mother would actually try to kill Vern again. "But regardless of who should get the blame for this clusterfuck, I'm not going to lie to help you out of this mess."

"Oh, you'll get your share of the blame, bitch. I'm not going down alone. I'll make sure everyone knows you were on board with this plan," Robert said in a tone Darlene had heard all too often lately. Was he threatening her again?

"Then I'll just have to take my lumps, but I'm not going to go along with any of your schemes anymore. I grew up with a scheming, conniving mother and traded her for the likes of you. It's time for me to play it straight," Darlene said with a resolve she hadn't felt in a long time—maybe ever.

"Good luck with that. I know you, Darlene. You'll never be satisfied with a nine to five job and a mundane existence. You'll always be looking for a way to score the big bucks and live the glamorous life."

"You really don't know me, Robert. All I've ever wanted was love and acceptance and I followed you down the wrong path hoping I'd get that from you. And it seems in the end you neither love nor accept me—just like my God damn mother." Darlene's voice cracked and a tear rolled down her cheek. "I can't do this anymore." Her phone vibrated with her words. A text was coming in.

"Are you getting another call?" Robert asked. "I heard your phone. Who are you talking to?"

"It's probably my mom." Darlene said. "I gotta go. I'll see you in court tomorrow, then when I get back to Seattle, I'll move my stuff out of your place."

"Really? We're breaking up on the phone? Can you at least see me?"

"No, I can't afford a black eye or a punch in the gut. Those days are over. Goodbye, Robert." She pressed the button to end the call before he could say another word.

The text was not from her mother. It was from Will telling her not to answer any calls from her mother's phone until he talked to her—he was on his way. She could do that. Why would she want to talk to her mother at this point? What more was there to say? The conversation with Robert reminded her so vividly that Gladys Dunwoody had been a poor excuse for a mother. It was time heal the scars of her childhood and move forward.

Will Fuller was on his way with some news. Had her mom gone through with her plan to rid the world of Vern Bradley? And why would Will tell her not to answer any calls from her mother or, for that matter, anyone in Puerto Vallarta.

Whatever the news, she knew she needed to wipe the mascara stain from her cheek, freshen her makeup, and spray a fresh burst of perfume in her hair. Looking in the mirror, she wondered how she had allowed Robert to batter her self-esteem. With cascading blonde curls framing her face and her violet-blue eyes staring back at her, she knew that even in her late thirties, she was still beautiful.

****

Will took a deep breath and knocked. When Darlene opened the door, she took that breath away. How would he find the words to tell her what happened? He could barely muster a "Hello, Darlene."

"Hi, Will. What did you find out? Did the cops track down my mother and Vern?"

"Yeah, they found them." He walked into the room, guiding Darlene to the couch by the window. The view of San Francisco from Nob Hill was incredible, but he wasn't looking out the window. His eyes were fixed on Darlene.

"So, you'll win your first case. Your client will be free to go, and we can all go on with our lives." Darlene smiled. "That's great news."

"Well, there's a little more to the story than that." He kept his gaze fixed on Darlene's beautiful eyes. "They found them five stories below their balcony—dead."

"Both of them?"

"Yes. Your mom is gone, Darlene. I'm sorry I had to be the one to tell you." He reached for her hand.

"Oh my God!" Darlene blinked several times. "I'm supposed to cry now, aren't I? I can't do it. I'm so mad at my mom for dying." She raised her voice. "Did she ever give a damn about me? I begged her to hug me the last time I saw her, and she just pushed me away—said I was too needy. Damn right I was needy. I needed my mom, and she was never there for me. Damn her. Damn her to hell." Darlene hung her head but still didn't shed a tear.

Will scooted close to her on the couch and put his arm around her. She leaned in, flung her arms around his neck, and held on. Will felt her heartbeat then a shudder—the tears would come next, and he would be here to hold her for as long as she needed him.

****

Darlene woke up hours later, still wrapped in Will's embrace. Crying herself to sleep hadn't been her intention, but the comfort she felt in his arms gave her a sense of peace. She couldn't remember the last time a man had hugged her without expecting sex.

"Are you feeling any better?" Will asked.

"A little. I'm going to bed. Would you stay and hold me tonight? I don't want to be alone."

"I'll stay with you," Will said. "I'm here for you."

Those simple words were all she'd ever wanted or needed. Maybe she'd finally found someone who would really be there for her.

Chapter Thirty-Six

Judgement Day

Facing the judge was a formality at this point. Clearly Jack Madison had not killed Vern Bradley and now, with the report from the Puerto Vallarta police, it had been determined that Vern had been the victim of his own plot to kill Gladys. With his prints on the screwdriver and a few loose screws on the balcony railing, there was no other logical conclusion.

In a few minutes, Will would present his findings to Judge Stone and the charges against Jack Madison would be dismissed. Walking down the hallway toward the courtroom, he felt Darlene reach for his hand—would he win both his case and the girl? He could tell she wouldn't be easy, but he saw something in her that told him she was worth the effort.

Outside the courtroom door, they caught up with Jack and Mary. Jack waved Will down and rushed toward him. Wrapping him in hug so tight it nearly squeezed the air out of Will's lungs, Jack choked on his words.

"Thank you for calling this morning to let me know Vern made it off the ship. With Robert's story and the pressure he put on me after the incident, I was beginning to think I was guilty."

Mary wrapped her arm around Jack. "You're

probably regretting marrying into my family. I'm so sorry you had to go through this, dear."

"I'll never be sorry I married you," Jack said as he kissed her cheek.

Mary leaned into Jack. "The one bright spot in all this is that Vern's life insurance will pay, and I'll get a hefty cut as a payoff for my interest in his business."

"I wish that were true," Will said, "but it seems Vern was in the act of committing murder—a felony—which is clearly stated in the insurance policy as an exclusion."

"I've known Vern most of my life," Mary said. "He's an asshole and an abuser, but I never thought he'd actually try to kill someone."

"That's because he didn't try to kill Gladys. It was the other way around," Robert chimed in. He'd been standing nearby, obviously eavesdropping. "Just ask Darlene. Her mother told her she was going to get rid of Vern, didn't she, Darlene?"

"I don't recall my mother saying anything of the sort," Darlene said.

"You know your mother is the guilty one. Are you going to screw us all out of five million dollars to save your mother's reputation? She's dead. And, you know this isn't her first attempt at killing my father," Robert said.

Darlene laughed in his face. "Consider yourself screwed. The evidence points to Vern and, frankly, he deserves the blame for all the shit we've been through."

Robert's face was turning red with his anger and when he saw Darlene holding Will's hand, he exploded. "She's all yours, Will. Good luck keeping her happy and when she turns on you, don't say I didn't warn you." He turned toward the courtroom door and walked inside.

Will smiled a half smile wondering what he'd gotten himself into. Then he looked at Darlene and figured it was worth a try. God, she was beautiful. "So, are we all ready to go inside and get the judge's take on all this?"

"I'm ready," Jack said as he reached for Mary's hand.

"I'm more than ready to put this chapter of my life behind me," Darlene said as she turned her eyes to Will and squeezed his hand. "I may just relocate after I sell my mom's condo in Puerto Vallarta. I'm her only living relative so I guess it's all mine."

Will turned to Jack and Mary. "Why don't you two go get settled inside. I'll be there in a minute." As they moved out of earshot, he pulled Darlene aside. "Are you telling me that condo is in your mother's name?"

Darlene smiled. "That was the plan. Vern was supposed to be dead, so he bought the condo and put it in my mom's name. He was all set to change his identity and live out his golden years in Puerto Vallarta with my mom and her share of the five million."

Will's mouth was hanging wide open. "Is there anything else you're not telling me? I'm sorry you won't get a share of that big payout, but I'm glad you decided to tell the truth and walk away from that life."

"A girl has to have a few secrets," Darlene said. "But I can tell you my mom had a small life insurance policy and I'm sure I'm the secondary beneficiary. Vern was first, of course. The men in her life always took priority over me but look at me now." Her voice was almost giddy.

Will wondered again what kind of a woman he might be getting involved with, but then he remembered her tears last night. It was only fitting that Gladys and

Robert, her two abusers—both emotional and physical—would end up with nothing and she would somehow be repaid for her dysfunctional life. There was hope for her, he thought.

****

"Will, it's almost two o'clock. Are you ready to defend me?" Jack said as he pulled Will away from Darlene. "What are you two doing out here?"

Jack was anxious to clear his name and didn't want to wait another moment. After he'd settled Mary into her seat behind the defense table with a kiss and a pat on the thigh, he'd run back out in the hallway to retrieve Will from Darlene's clutches. Knowing Will was a bright young man, he wondered if he was only book smart and not so bright when it came to women. Jack had come to think of Will almost like a son and he wished he could protect him, but in the end, young Will would have to make his own mistakes.

"I'm coming," Will said as he dropped Darlene's hand and caught up to Jack. The two men, so many years apart, were not so different when it came to understanding women. Jack just happened to get lucky when he found Mary.

Will and Jack took their seats at the defense table with Mary and Darlene close behind them. Watching Dick Diamond saunter to the chair he occupied at so many of his winning trials, Jack smiled knowing this was one "The Dick" couldn't win.

Listening to the words of the bailiff for the last time, Jack could barely contain his joy. "All rise for the honorable Judge Alexis Stone."

"You may be seated," Judge Stone said as she rapped her gavel. "We are here this morning to determine whether the victim, Vern Bradley, is still alive. What did you discover after contacting the authorities, Mr. Fuller?"

"Your Honor, Vern Bradley is not alive, but his death is not as a result of a fall overboard on *The Queen of the Seas*. Vern Bradley's body was found yesterday morning next to his girlfriend, Gladys Dunwoody, five stories below the balcony of their condominium. It appears Mr. Bradley had loosened the screws on the railing in what appears to be an attempt to murder Ms. Dunwoody. Somehow it must have gone awry, and they both fell to their death. I have the police report right here," Will said with a smile that Jack mimicked as they both looked over at Dick Diamond, then back to the judge.

"Counsel, please approach the bench."

Will and Dick Diamond both moved forward, Will with his report in hand.

Jack watched as Judge Stone read the report and spoke to both attorneys, then sent them back to their seats.

"In view of the report in my hand, it is clear that Jack Madison did not kill Vern Bradley. So, first of all, I would like to place Robert Bradley in custody for perjury as we now know he could not have seen his father fall over the railing. I'm showing leniency in your case, Mr. Bradley, since, from the look on your face, you did not know your father was actually dead. My condolences along with six months' probation. We will assign you a probation officer in Seattle." The judge smiled as she turned her attention to Jack. "Mr. Madison, it makes me very happy to say all charges against you will be erased from your record and you are free to go." She lifted her gavel. "Case dismissed!" At the sound of the gavel hitting the wood, Will and Jack stood up, hugged, and looked over the rail at their women.

"Thank you, Will." Jack practically shouted the words. "How can I ever repay you?"

"Oh, your son-in-law took care of that nicely. I'm just glad I earned my fee." Will put his arm around Jack and delivered him to Mary. "Good luck to both of you. Now go back to Seattle and finish your honeymoon." Jack hugged Mary so tight she squealed.

"Will, I can't thank you enough for giving me back my husband." Mary hugged Will. "Pardon us if we don't hang around, but we've got plane reservations to make. You take care of yourself." Mary winked and nodded toward Darlene. "We'll miss you, but we hope we never need you again."

"I understand," Will said. "I'm glad you were my first defendant, Jack."

"I couldn't have asked for a better defense." Jack gave him one last hug then grabbed Mary's hand and literally skipped out of the courtroom.

When he got to the hallway, all the family that could be there—Jamie, Sam, Justin, and Annie—were waiting to congratulate Jack. Texts from Sarah and voicemail from Aunt Dot sent his joy meter over the top. There had been a few bumps in the road with his family, but today he felt the love of each and every one of them. Did he deserve all this love and attention? Maybe and maybe not, but he was damn sure he would do everything in his power to earn their love and respect for the rest of his life. He was one lucky guy. Squeezing Mary's hand, he gazed into her emerald-green eyes, remembering how beautiful she'd looked in her silky white dress on the

bow of the ship when she said "I do."
And, then he kissed her…

A word about the author...

Jacquie May Miller published her first article at age eleven in her neighborhood newspaper, the Nosy Neighborhood News. She continued her writing journey many years later when she created May Daze, a blog exploring the value of friendship, family, and life's little surprises. You will find her at www.jmaydaze.com where she has attracted a loyal following.

DO YOU TAKE THIS MAN? is Jacquie's second novel, a sequel to THE PRICE OF SECRETS.

While Jacquie's first novel leaves no dead or missing bodies, DO YOU TAKE THIS MAN? cannot make that promise as it explores a darker side of life in a mystery at sea. Ride along on The Queen of the Seas for a journey of mischief, mayhem and maybe a murder or two...

Jacquie lives in Washington close to her only child, Brittney, who is the light of her life.
http://www.jmaydaze.com